THIS
IS
NOT
FORGIVE-
NESS

THIS
IS
NOT
FORGIVE-
NESS

Celia Rees

BLOOMSBURY

NEW YORK LONDON NEW DELHI SYDNEY

First published in Great Britain in February 2012 by Bloomsbury Publishing Plc
Published in the United States of America in October 2012
by Bloomsbury Books for Young Readers
www.bloomsburyteens.com

For information about permission to reproduce selections from this book, write to
Permissions, Bloomsbury BFYR, 175 Fifth Avenue, New York, New York 10010

The publishers are grateful to the following for permission
to reproduce copyright material:

Lines from 'My Brother's Vespa', *Selected Poems*, by Peter Sansom © 2010,
published by Carcanet Press

Lines from 'Pirate Jenny', *The Threepenny Opera*, by Bertolt Brecht,
translated by Ralph Manheim and John Willett, Methuen Drama, an
imprint of Bloomsbury Publishing Plc, translation copyright © 1979 Brecht
Heirs, original work entitled *Die Dreigroschenoper* © 1928 Gustav
Kiepenheuer Verlag, renewed 1968 by Helene Brecht-Weigel

Library of Congress Cataloging-in-Publication Data
Rees, Celia.
This is not forgiveness / by Celia Rees. — 1st U.S. ed.
        p.   cm.
Summary: In England, a beautiful, manipulative teenaged girl affiliated
with a group of political anarchists seduces both seventeen-year-old Jamie
and his older brother, a wounded veteran of the war in Afghanistan.
ISBN 978-1-59990-776-5 (hardcover)
[1. Love—Fiction. 2. Brothers—Fiction. 3. Emotional problems—Fiction.
4. Terrorism—Fiction.] I. Title.
PZ7.R25465Th 2012   [Fic]—dc23   2012005204

Typeset by Hewer Text UK Ltd, Edinburgh
Printed in the U.S.A. by Quad/Graphics, Fairfield, Pennsylvania
2 4 6 8 10 9 7 5 3 1

For Colwyn Morris (1921–2011)
Artist, sharpshooter, Desert Rat

First we live
then we remember.

My Brother's Vespa
Peter Sansom

I can't decide what to do with your ashes. It's been nearly a year now. Almost summer again. The urn is sitting in front of me on the desk, brown plastic with a ref. number, the date and your name scribbled on a sticky label:

Robert Julian Maguire

The label has black borders and is beginning to peel at the corners. I smooth the wrinkled paper, trying to stick it back. It has been slapped on crooked by someone who didn't care a whole lot about the contents. There are all kinds of urns you can have: brass, copper, pewter, ceramic; you can have a wooden casket with engraving on it, but those cost and someone would have to care enough to order one and buy it. I guess yours is the modern equivalent of the pauper's grave.

I went to the funerals. They held them one after another. I don't think they meant them to be that way, but the crematorium was busy that day. Yours was second. Not much like the first. No orations, no weeping school mates clutching single blossoms to put on the coffin, sobbing out rubbish verses that they'd written themselves. No inky hand-printed notes on the flowers: *R.I.P.*, *C U in Heaven*, *Gone but not forgotten.* No flowers at all. Hardly anyone there, either. Only the bare minimum for decency. Police and immediate family. Some of your mates, but not many. Just Bryn and a few others, wearing uniform.

The priest was sweating. He kept dabbing at his forehead with a big white handkerchief and stumbling over his words, scratching about to find something to say, stringing it out until the time came for the rollers to engage. You would have pissed yourself. Nobody sang the hymn, there was just this tinny recording. Nobody cried or even looked sad. The congregation seemed relieved to see your coffin going, as if it wasn't a body on its way to the furnace but some dangerous biohazard. They couldn't wait to get out of there.

I was the one who went back to collect your ashes. That's how I've got them here. Mum doesn't like it. She keeps nagging about 'disposal' and 'closure'. Keeping you here is morbid and probably unhealthy. I don't see it. The Morgans had their granddad on the mantelpiece for years and years. She wants rid, but what's it to do with her? You were my brother. She doesn't have to come in here. 'It's

2

upsetting for your sister,' she says. I know for a fact that Martha couldn't give a monkey's fat one. Anyway, she's not even here, so what does she care?

I can see Mum's point of view. What you did was pretty disruptive. I had to move schools. I couldn't go back there, could I? Mum wanted to move house. Move towns. After what happened, she wanted to make a fresh start. You've made the place toxic. But in the end, we didn't do that. We'd have had to move Grandpa. Not that he'd notice. He's still alive, just about, but Alzheimer's doesn't get better, does it?

It wasn't really that, either. What happened has changed her. At times, she blames herself. Somehow it must be her fault, that's what she thinks. If she'd just done this thing, or that thing, then it wouldn't have happened. She spends a lot of time sitting around thinking about that. She's there but not there when she's like that. She moves from that to being very, very angry. Mostly with you.

Maybe getting rid of you would give us closure, as she puts it, but I don't think so. The brown plastic kind of contains you. Without it, you'd be everywhere – like a genie. You don't deserve to be liberated yet. I'll decide the time and place. It could be tomorrow, it could be years from now, but until the day comes, you are staying right here, with me.

But this is not forgiveness. Don't think that.

Over in Afghan lots of guys make some kind of statement before they go on ops – especially if there's a chance they might not be coming back. They write an email or a letter or a crap poem – whatever. Or make a podcast – like this one.

I never did that. Asking for it in my opinion.

Inviting bad luck.

Now luck ain't coming into it – I'm doing this because I don't want no misunderstanding. I'm not like those sad-loner no-mates fucks against the world – there's no chip on my shoulder. Don't be looking to blame anyone – clean up the mess and get on with your lives.

I want you all to know I didn't do it as some kind of personal declaration – I don't have a message.

My only cause is me.

And I ain't crazy. That'd be too easy.

Don't look for reasons because there are no reasons. But people want them don't they – so take your pick from these:

I was tired of living in Snoreton-on-Boring with no future that I can see.

I was sick of the ordinary and wanted to stir up the ant heap.

I wanted to make people take notice. Nothing concentrates the mind like death and dying, does it?

Don't ask 'Why?' cos that's the wrong question.

Better to ask 'Why not?'

It's amazing that this don't happen

ALL THE TIME!

3

The Rendez

I come here with my laptop. It's a way to get back to the time that is in my mind, the time that I've set myself to write about. Jesse keeps me supplied with coffee. We're friends now. She'd like us to be more, but it's too soon for that. The place is full of mirrors. Sometimes I look up and don't recognise myself. I began the account as a letter to my brother. I might change my mind about that.

It's last July. We're here in this place you don't like because you think it's poncy and full of arseholes. It's four o'clock on a Friday, after school anyway, so you're probably down Wetherspoon's having a few pints. I'm here with Cal. We were best mates then. Friends since nursery but that was about to change. Had been changing, if I'm honest. I'd just failed to notice. We are talking about you. Cal was scared of you when we were little, although he liked to claim you in the playground. Your name being enough to keep the bullies at bay. He never did say all that much when he met you, just 'Hi. How's it going?'. That could be because you pretty much ignored him, even when he was scoring off you. In his head, Cal reckons he's a bit of a bad boy, likes to think he has attitude, but he's the opposite, his credentials are nil. He wouldn't do shit, but he's fascinated by those who do.

While he talks, which he does all the time, I'm looking around for diversion and thinking, maybe you're right. This cafe *is* poncy and full of arseholes. It's called the *Rendez* for a start. Short for *Rendezvous*.

It's supposed to be kind of French, with worn wooden tables, the walls crowded with big mirrors, posters and photographs. Old adverts for different kinds of drink: Guinness, Pernod, Coca-Cola. Photographs full of dead people. Street scenes. Staff paraded outside stores that have gone now. How the town used to be. The mirrors are rippled and pockmarked, the silvery reflections they give back smeared by time. I like mirrors. They're a useful way to watch people; to watch people watching themselves.

That's what I'm doing. I'm watching people in the mirrors. That's how I first see her and I'm no longer listening to Cal. She's sitting with an older woman, there's enough of a resemblance to know that it's her mother, and a bunch of other women who look like her mother's friends. They are getting stuck into the wine, but she's sipping a Diet Coke through a straw, clinking the ice in the glass, looking around like she's bored. There's a younger lad with her, probably her brother, munching his way through a bowl of chunky chips, dunking them first in ketchup, then mayo, so the mayo is getting red and messy, like it's streaked with blood. Sometimes he offers the bowl over, like they are supposed to be sharing, but she just waves him away. He's a little on the chunky side himself, so he looks relieved. The women ignore them, too busy with each other. They are getting down the bottle now, ordering another, their laughter is getting louder the further down the bottle they go. When one is empty, a waitress comes over with a replacement.

The girls who work here are fit. It might not be enough to get Rob in here, I'm thinking, but it works for me and Cal. That's one of the reasons we've started coming in here, that and the fact that Cal's girlfriend, Sophie, comes here with her mates. She thinks it's *the* place to be, so naturally Cal thinks that, too. I realise that's why we are here. I'm just a time-filler. He's arranged to meet Sophie.

I wonder what the girl sees in the mirror? Two boys drinking coffee. I'm the one on the right: dark, thicker set, hair cut short, neat. Her eyes move to Cal. He's a different prospect. Most girls go for him. He pushes a hand through his hair. It won't be long before he looks in the mirror. I expect her to carry on looking at him, but she dismisses him and turns her gaze on me. That's when I look away. Don't want her to think I've been staring. I know her. One of Martha's friends, or ex-friends, more like, cos I haven't seen her for a while now. She shows no sign of recognition. Maybe she doesn't remember me.

'Has he?' Cal is asking.

'Has he what?'

'Got any stuff? I need some draw. You haven't been listening. Who's she?'

'Who's who?'

'That girl you've been staring at.'

'Her name's Vanessa. Used to be a friend of Martha's.'

'Vanessa *Carrington*?'

'Yes, as it happens. They call her Caro.'

'So *that's* her. She's *hot!*'

He checks her out, automatically messing with his hair as he does so and putting on his best pulling smile. She gives a look to freeze us both out.

'How do you know about her?' I ask.

'Sophie told me.'

'Oh, yeah. What did she say?'

'Just she's got quite a rep. She'd be too much for you, mate. You couldn't even handle Suzy . . .'

He gives me a look of pure pity. He's been giving me that particular look since Suzy dumped me. He didn't consider her much of a girlfriend, not compared to the blonde divinity who is Sophie. She'd never go out on double dates with us because she thought I was too dull and Suzy was too ordinary. Suze is all right now. She's bought an iPhone and hair straighteners and doesn't shop in River Island any more. She's in. I'm out.

Fine by me. I preferred her when she was ordinary and I don't like Sophie. She's Cal's first real girlfriend, the first one who'd let him screw her, anyway. Now, he can't get enough. I hardly see him. If I do, he's using me as a fill in, like now. *He* reckons it's love. Perhaps it is. What would I know? They're applying to the same universities. They'll be like one of those student couples going round Sainsbury's together, the girl piling up the veggies, turfing out the pizzas and swapping six-packs for spring water while the guy troops along behind her, lugging the basket, miserable as fuck.

'You're pussy-whipped, mate. Everybody says it.' I laugh, getting my own back.

'Who says it?'

'Everybody,' I repeat. 'Everybody we know.'

He looks a little bit disconcerted but it doesn't take long for him to rally.

'*Au contraire*, my friend. She's ruled by this.' He thrusts his hips, his low slung jeans bunched and rucked as if he kept something huge down there. I grin at him. I know the reality. 'You're just jealous because you're not getting any.'

There's truth in that.

His face changes to serious. He used to be funny. Not any more. As if on cue, Sophie appears. She's outside,

11

saying goodbye to her mates. She waves to Cal through the window. Suzy is with her. Looks straight through me as if she's never seen me before in her life. There's a lot of hugging and kissing, squealy farewells and hair tossing. It's as if Sophie is going on a gap year, not coming in here for a coffee.

Caro shifts her gaze. She looks at them and looks away. Sophie comes in, arms outstretched. She flits past me and puts her arms round Cal, kissing him and calling him baby, like she's in some budget version of *The Hills*. She sits at the table and carries on the baby talk. I'm ignored.

'Hi, Sophie,' I say.

'Oh, hi,' she says and looks at me as though I'm some kind of uncool pet, like a staffy or a pit bull puppy, then carries on talking to Cal, telling him what an epic day she's had.

'I'm off, then.' I stand up. 'Nice seeing you, Sophie.'

'Yeah, bye,' she says and I'm dismissed with a slight wave of her hand. The wristbands and ratty little friendship bracelets she's wearing reach halfway to her elbow.

'I'll get this.' I nod at Cal, who nods back. He smiles but he has this look in his eyes. Lost and terrified. Sophie's voice loses the baby tone, becomes brisker, more business like. Cal goes to say something but she's not listening. He tries again. The same thing. He glances over her shoulder, as if to gauge the distance to the door.

Too late for that, mate, I think as I wait for the till. *You want to screw her! It's the price you have to pay!*

I'm glad it's not me.

I'm so busy thinking that, and laughing to myself, that I don't really notice until I'm standing behind her that Caro is there, too, queuing while her mother buys stuff from the deli counter. She's wearing a thin vest top and the strap has slipped. There's a star tattooed on her left shoulder. The tattoo is very dark sepia, almost black, like a pattern burnt into wood. Each point of the star is filled with little dots and marks. Her back is tanned a golden colour and spattered with freckles. Her skin looks soft, warm and supple. Her dark hair is cut in a chin-length bob, it gives her a kind of sixties look. It moves as she turns her head and is very shiny, like it would feel slippery through your fingers . . .

She puts a hand up to her shoulder and twists round as if she feels my look like a touch. Her hair swings back and I see her in profile, close, just for a camera-shutter fraction of time, then the hair falls like a curtain and she is moving away.

'Bye, Caro,' the girl behind the till says, and she turns back for a moment, giving her a fleeting smile.

I stand there, wishing the smile had been for me. She follows her mother and brother to the door. I should have said something, spoken to her. Although what could I have said? *Don't I know you from somewhere?* I shake my head. That would sound such a line. No other words readily spring to mind. Too late now, anyway.

She's gone and I might not see her again. At that moment, seeing her again seems like the most important thing in the world.

'Reel your tongue back in,' the girl behind the till says and gives me a look, two parts pity to one part sympathy with just a dash of mockery. 'Do you know her? Caro?'

'Not really, er . . .' I shrug, start to blush.

'You're Martha Maguire's brother, aren't you?' She smiles.

That's me slotted. Martha's brother. Cal's friend.

'Yeah,' I say, 'I'm Jamie.'

She's pretty with a husky voice and long, curly hair and piercings everywhere. Her name is Jesse. She used to go to primary with Martha, used to come round our house to play. This is a small town.

'Thought I knew you. That'll be £2.50, Jamie.' She hands me the bill folded on a china saucer. 'Unless you're paying for him, too, in which case it's £5.' I lay a note on the plate, then add 50p as a tip, my mind still running on the girl who has just walked out of the door. I want to know more about her. I want to know *all* about her. Martha will be able to tell me. Martha keeps tabs on people.

'Thanks,' I say, not sure what I'm thanking her for.

'No worries,' Jesse smiles again. 'All part of the service.'

Her smile fades as she watches Caro stalk past the

window heading towards a Mini convertible parked at the kerb.

'Good luck with that.' She adds as Caro climbs into the driver's seat and slams the door.

4

'*And they'll ask: which of these should we kill?*
In that noonday heat there'll be a hush round the harbour
As they ask which has got to die.
And you'll hear me as I softly answer: the lot!'
'*Pirate Jenny*' – Bertolt Brecht and Kurt Weill,
'*The Threepenny Opera*'

Pirate Jenny. It's a game I play. A game in which I choose who gets it and who doesn't. It passes the time.

I'm sitting in the Rendez *with my mother and her friends. Everyone calls it that.* Rendez – *short for the* Rendezvous. *Trying hard to be French: worn wooden tables, big mirrors,* pot au feu *on the chalked-up menu. The mirrors are the real thing, not repro. I spend a lot of time looking into them, so I should know. They make the place look darker, more mysterious; they make people look glamorous. They might not reflect reality but they're good for picking out victims.*

My mother meets her friends here to drink wine and gossip. I don't usually come with her, but tonight I couldn't get out of it. She's done something for me, so now I have to do something for her. Quid pro quo. She's been with me to the new school I've got to attend. We've been to see the Principal: Armani suit, fancies himself. Fancies me, too, from the way he's checking me out. And my mother. Bit of a sleazebag, then. Just a preliminary chat, see if we like each other. *Cue: hearty laugh as his eyes switch from her legs to my cleavage.*

'I have to have a drink after that.' She gives a mock shudder when we're out of his office. 'Let's go to the Rendez.' She says it like it's an original and new idea. 'My friends are dying to see you.'

That's what she says, although it's not true. Her friends have no interest in me. She really wants me here because I can drive, so she can drink as much as she likes.

My stepbrother is here, too. We picked him up from his after-school club. I'm sipping a Diet Coke. He's working his way through a big bowl of chips. We don't speak to each other and Mother and her friends ignore us. She's got lots of friends. Networking, she calls it, and she's good at it.

All her friends are on my list.

They hardly register my presence. They get on with the everlasting conversation about how crap their lives are, or their jobs, or their husbands, or their boyfriends, or any combination or lack of the above. That's all they ever talk about. My mother is sitting in profile. She chats, laughing and smiling, or nods with her head on one side in listening mode. Every now and again she twists to check herself out in the mirror and sees me there.

18

Mirror, mirror on the wall. . .

Not you, Mother dear. Not any more.

I catch her look: jealousy mixed with admiration. I'm also here as her appendage. She's been toting me about since I was tiny – I was a cute-looking child. She likes to show me off to her friends. Not so much recently. She's beginning to feel the competition. But I'm not looking at her, or even at myself. I'm looking at the two boys. The dark one is Jamie Maguire. Martha's brother. I don't know the other one but I've seen him around. Jamie isn't bad in a dull kind of way. He's wearing a blue pull-over and jeans, like his mum still buys his clothes. I think that's rather sweet. The waitress arrives with their coffee. I know her, too. Jesse. The blond begins flirting with her, looking up through his long lashes. Jesse smiles back, indulgent, but she isn't having any. She's more interested in Jamie, but the blond guy can't see it. He's not used to girls saying 'no'. He looks like an Abercrombie and Fitch model. The jeans aren't cheap, the rest of his outfit is High Street, but well put together. Tatty tennis shoes strictly model's own. He rakes a hand through his dirty blond hair. It won't be long before he checks himself in the mirror. There he goes, quick look to see that his hair's OK. Boys like him are obsessed with themselves. More than girls. Narcissism repels me. He goes on my list.

Jamie doesn't. I like a plain canvas.

He glances up, too, as if he senses my thought and

19

he's not looking at himself, he's looking at me. Not for the first time, either, I've been noticing him, noticing me. The blond shifts his gaze ever so slightly, to check out what his friend is checking out, and then they are both staring. My mother catches them and thinks they are looking at her. She would, wouldn't she? She kind of simpers and I think that she is going to wink, or wave, tip her drink, or do something equally embarrassing. I should be colouring, but I never blush. I just look away.

There are girls outside the window. I know a few of them. The tall blonde peels off and comes in to join Jamie and his friend. Our Jamie looks pissed off. She doesn't look too pleased to see him, either.

I'd have liked to have watched them longer, I like watching people, but Roland has finished his chips and has started to complain. Roland, Rollo, the kid really lives up to his name. He puts up with all kinds of shit at school because of it, but he's OK. He's not on my list.

The friends are set to make a night of it. My mother would love to stay, but knows she can't. Her smile slips for a moment. There is a flicker of annoyance and resentment before she says, 'Of course, sweetie. Time to go, anyway.'

We get up to go and pay at the counter. My mother blows kisses and mouthes 'Call me', little finger and thumb extended towards her ear, but her friends have turned away to carry on their conversation. It's as though we have already left.

We wait while she orders stuff from the deli counter. Jamie is behind me; standing close, too close. I can feel his breath on my neck, but I don't move away. He's improved since I last saw him. Even though I know him, I blank him. He doesn't say anything, either. That's how it is in this town.

A weird thing has just happened. I opened a drawer to put my notebook back, and there's my pack of tarot cards. I didn't notice them before. I didn't even think they were in that drawer. I don't believe in any of that stuff any more. All that divination crap belongs to my goth/emo phase. That was all just kids' stuff. I'm into something much bigger now, swapped astrology for agitprop, but I used to be deeply into that kind of shit. I liked all the paraphernalia, the charts, the runes, the tarot, the crystal.

My favourite thing was the planchette. I got it on a junk stall. Victorian, carved out of ebony. It is shaped like a heart and runs on three little casters. At the pointed end, there is a place to fix a pencil. So much better than a Ouija board but not enormous fun on your own. That's one of the reasons I started the Circle. We used to meet at my house, paint our fingernails black, apply weird make-up, dye our hair indigo and dabble in the occult while listening to Bikini Kill, Beth Ditto, Free Kitten and Lady Gaga before anyone else liked her.

The Circle didn't last long, though.

She will peak and she will pine . . .

Those spells I found on the Internet were so cheesy. Never thought for a moment that they would actually work. You can get spells for almost everything. Martha's spots and hair loss were a laugh, no more than she deserved, but Louise Simpson on life support? That scared the shit out of them. The Circle broke up after that. I was getting bored with it, anyway. At the moment when the spells we were weaving actually seemed to be working, I ceased believing. Ironic that. But then, that's how I am.

Occult paraphernalia, leached of their power, become mere knick-knacks. The planchette sits on my desk now – just an interesting objet. The rune stones look pretty on the windowsill. And the tarot? Doesn't everybody own a pack of tarot cards?

I take them out of my drawer. I have to admit that I still feel a bit of a tug. A little thrill.

I cut, shuffle, cut again. Just for old time's sake. I find him there. The Fool. It doesn't mean bozo, just someone innocent but wise at the same time. The Creative Dreamer. It's him. Got to be. I feel some of the old excitement stirring inside me.

He was in my mind, I'd just been writing about him, so I would see him, wouldn't I? That's how it works.

I cut again. The Knave of Swords. The Berserker. The archetypal warrior. That's interesting. Now I've got the two of them. *Jamie and his brother. I'm curious so I cut again. Queen of Swords reversed: devious, underhand, expert in the use of half-truths and slander. That* has *to be Martha.*

5

'Come in, if you're coming in.'

Martha doesn't look round from where she's wielding her hair straighteners. She has long hair and it takes her ages. She has to do it every morning. She sets her alarm an hour early just to get ready for school. One of the things that make me glad that I'm not female. Everything takes so long. I don't know why she does that to her hair. Mum reckons it's bad for it, making it thin. Martha was having problems with that a while ago, around the time of her GCSEs. The doctor put it down to stress. It seems all right now, although I prefer it when she leaves it curly. So does Mum, but Martha doesn't take any notice of us. She thinks I'm clueless and that Mum just wants her to stay a little girl.

'Whatever it is, make it quick. I've still got my make-up to do and the girls will be here in a minute for pre-drinks.' She puts down the straighteners and rummages through her make-up case.

'I was just wondering. . .' I wander in and start looking at stuff on her table, squaring up her books.

'Leave it! Don't touch! Sit!' She orders me about as though I'm still six. There's only a bit more than a year between us, but she acts like she's the only one who has grown up. 'You were wondering what?'

'You know that girl, the one they call Caro? She's got a tattoo here.' I reach round and touch my shoulder. 'Shaped like a star with squiggles in it.'

'If you mean Vanessa Carrington, then yes, I know her. And that's not a star. It's a pentacle and those aren't squiggles, they're sigils. You're such a dick!'

I don't know what sigils are but I'm not about to ask her and prove I'm even more stupid and ignorant than she believes me to be. I look the word up later – an occult symbol or device supposed to have magical powers.

'What about her?' Martha doesn't look at me. She is applying mascara in careful, slow, upward sweeps.

'Well, what's she like? I mean . . .'

'Why do you want to know?'

'Oh, um, me and Cal saw her in the *Rendez*.'

'And?'

'We were just . . .' I shrug. 'You know . . . interested.'

'Cal? I thought he'd got a girlfriend. Insufferable Sophie.'

'Well, yes . . .'

26

'He doesn't want another one, surely? I thought they were in *lurve*.'

'They are. He thinks, anyway.'

'So, it's *you*, then. You are the one who is *interested*.'

'Er, yes. I guess. I was just wondering. I mean, didn't you two used to be friends?'

'Long time ago. Not any more, we aren't.' She puts down the mascara and swings round to face me, one eye big, the other one small. The effect is disconcerting. 'So if you were *wondering* do I have her number in my phone, the answer to that is . . . no. Sorry to disappoint you, little bro. Don't even think about going there. That girl is seriously *bad*.'

'Really? She looked all right to me.'

'You can't tell by looking, can you?' She starts on the other eye. 'Not what you'd be looking at, anyway. She's a real troublemaker – involved in some *pretty* bad stuff.'

I'm even more intrigued, but she doesn't go into exact details about what that 'bad stuff' might be. She's keen to tell me something else. 'She's just been chucked out of school.'

'Really? What for?'

'For being an über bitch and über slag, quite apart from all her other misdemeanours, that's what for.'

'What'd she do?'

'Had an affair with one of the teachers, who's since been sacked. She's got a thing for older guys. She'd eat you up, and not in a nice way.' She smiles at herself in the mirror, as if that idea amuses her. She turns her head this way and that to judge how her make-up is coming together. 'Now, how do I look?'

She stands up, shimmying her hips to release the flimsy, shiny material of her dress. She's got good legs. Long, slender and a golden brown colour. She's been at Mum's fake tan again. She's not wearing so much make-up since her skin cleared up. I like that. The natural look. Suits her better.

'Great!' I smile at her. Not that there is a choice, but I do mean it. 'You look pretty good.'

'Pretty good! Is that all you can come up with!' She turns back at herself in the mirror. 'I look bloody fantastic! That's the bell. It'll be the girls.' She's trying to put in earrings and get into her heels at the same time. 'You get it. Send 'em up. I've got some voddy, no, you can't have any, and don't stare at their tits when you let them in, or any other parts of their anatomy. Girls know what you are doing and it's embarrassing.'

It's hard not to notice. They are dressed for going out, which means low-cut and very short, but I manage to let them in with eyes averted. They've been to the corner shop on their way and come in supplied with half-bottles of Smirnoff. Martha's best buddies. Melissa, Sally and the other one, whose real name is Letitia but they call her Lee. She's a recent addition. Part of Martha's outreach work. She's quiet, not as flamboyant as the others. She's wearing ballet pumps and jeans, a white top and almost no make-up. The other two are tricked up like Pussycat Dolls.

They all go upstairs and Martha shouts down orders for glasses and ice and cranberry juice. I go to the kitchen and fetch what's needed: a bowl of ice, tall glasses, orange juice, cranberry and Coke, in case anyone wants a different mixer. I even find the packets of nuts, crisps and corn chips left over from the barbecue last weekend and shake them out into little dishes. I stack the lot on a tray, fold a tea cloth over my arm and mount the stairs.

I'm happy to play barman and waiter. I want to know more about this Caro and if Martha won't tell me, I'm betting one of the others will – especially after the hefty vodkas I'll be pouring for them tonight. I consider going to get a baggie from the stash Rob kindly bequeathed to me and rolling a spliff or two, but decide against it. Might be too much with the vodka. I don't want anyone passing out on me.

I'm not wrong. It doesn't take them long. All I have to do is say her name and they're off. The girls love to gossip and it seems that she has given them plenty to gossip about. Besides, they like having me around. They think I'm kind of cute, but more important than that, I've got male friends. That's enough for Mel and Sal.

Mel starts. 'Van the Maneater? She's left our school. I thought she'd gone to yours. She missed her A levels, so she'll have to repeat a year.'

'I haven't seen her about.'

Mel shrugs. 'Haven't heard anything from Joss and the others, come to think about it.' A lot of girls from their school transfer to ours. 'She's unlikely to have slipped under their radar. Maybe she dropped out. She doesn't like school.'

'Excuse me.' I pretend to be insulted. 'Sixth form college.'

'Same difference. Why do you want to know about her, anyway?'

'Just interested.'

Martha gives a snort, but doesn't interrupt.

Mel takes a quick draw on the cigarette she's holding and blows a thin stream of smoke out into the evening air. She and Sally have lit up and are puffing out of the window. I don't know why they bother. Smoking is a pure waste of money and they don't even do it properly. Martha doesn't like this. She clicks her long polished nails on the desk. She doesn't approve of smoking and she'll be thinking Mum will smell it. Mum's out right now. Gone to a barbecue with Jack, her partner. Martha is worried she'll know. She can pick up smoke of any kind. They could use her at the airport, instead of sniffer dogs. That was one of the sources of friction when Rob lived here. He was always in trouble for lighting up in the house.

'You watch yourself with her.' Mel takes another quick puff. 'They don't call her maneater for nothing. She did for Charlie at school.'

I look blank.

'Just-call-me-Charlie Hands, the Art teacher.'

I think I know who she means. He was part-time at our school for a while. Thirty-something but going for mid-twenties. Hair receding, what there is left in a bit of a fin, beard half a centimetre longer than stubble. Thinks he's pretty alternative. Wears combat and T-shirts to school and gets away with it because he's an Art teacher. Normal rules don't apply.

'So what happened?'

'Well, he's been sacked and she's been expelled. Should have got rid of her ages ago, if you ask me, after she was suspended for wagging school to go on that demo –'

'Day of action,' Martha corrects.

'Whatever.' Mel carries on, eager to continue the gossip. 'Anyway, the Head saw her on the news wearing a riot helmet and jumping all over a police van.'

'And what about when she sprayed anarchist signs all over the language lab wall?' Sal adds.

'No one proved that was her,' Lee points out.

'Who else is it gonna be?' Sal sneers back. 'Banksy?'

'What happened with this Charlie guy?' I ask, trying to get them back on topic. That's the story that interests me.

'Well . . .' Sal leans forward, eager to share. 'She was shagging him and – '

'He deserves sacking,' Martha says, 'and she deserves expelling. Little slag!'

'She's not the only one,' Mel points out. 'Remember that girl – what's-her-name Bridges? Went to Goldsmiths?

He was doing her for years. Still is. Goes to see her in London. Her sister told me.'

'Why didn't he get the sack for that?' I ask.

Mel shrugs. 'That time no one found out.'

'This time?'

'There was no hiding it,' Mel continues. 'There was this student teacher. Don. Gelled hair. Taught Geography. Fancied himself. He was hot for her as well. Hands totally lost it. They had a fight. A real brawl. In the dining room. Rolling about on the floor. Tables tipped up, plates flying, water jugs ditto, custard all over. The lot.'

Mel's eyes gleam at the memory.

'I missed it! I had netball practice.' Sally expresses real anguish.

A fight between members of staff in the dining room? I don't get why they dislike this girl. Members of staff fighting over her? At our place that'd be enough to make her legend.

The other one, Lee, pipes up. 'That wasn't how it happened,' she says. She's not as gobby as the others. Not shy, just contained inside herself. 'Caro wasn't doing anything with that student. He fancied her, that's all.'

'That's not what *we* heard,' Mel and Sal say together. Lee is deviating from the script, spoiling the fun.

'Caro didn't even fancy him. The student, I mean, and she knew Charlie out of school. They were putting on an art show.'

That sets Sal and Mel spluttering their drinks.

'Yeah, right! Getting it on, more like!'

'But it's all just gossip, isn't it? That's the trouble with our school.'

'So what were they fighting about, then?' I ask Lee.

I'm intrigued by why she's on Caro's side while the others dislike her. She looks at me from under her lashes. She's wary, wondering what my motive might be. I smile back, open-faced, innocent and friendly. Just chatting, that's all. I want her to go on. I want her to tell me more.

'The Geography student said something about her. Hands threw a jug of water over him. That's how the fight started.'

'And how do you know that?' Mel looks unbelieving because it just might be the truth.

'The other student, the one who teaches History, told me. She likes Caro. Doesn't think it's fair what happened to her.'

'The dykey one who wears a Stop the Cuts badge? Maybe she fancies her, too.' Mel smirks. 'Maybe she's another one of her conquests.' Her grin grows wider. 'Hey! Van the Muffeater!'

The others shriek and fall about, although it really isn't all that funny. Lee isn't laughing. She throws back her drink and reaches for Mel's pack of ten.

'Can I have one?' she asks, although she has already helped herself.

She lights the cigarette as a blind. She takes a long drag, taking the smoke down.

There's more to this one, I think, as she sucks on her cigarette and leans on the windowsill. The sleeve of her top slips a bit as she reaches forward to flick the ash. I don't see all of it, but I see enough to recognise the shape and colour on the white flesh of her shoulder: the dark burnt mark of the five-pointed star. She finishes her drink and Mel pours her another.

'Weren't you part of her coven?' Mel stubs her fag. 'Weren't you lot, like, doing *black magic*?' She says the words with a shudder and rolls her eyes, pulling a face like a drama mask. 'Putting spells on people?'

'It was nothing like that.' Lee is keen to play down the possibility. 'Just messing about, mostly. Don't believe everything you're told.'

'They say that Caro used *powers*,' Sal insists. 'That she put spells on people. Like Louise Simpson.'

They all nod as if they know the name.

'What happened to Louise Simpson?' I ask. They are losing me now.

'She ended up in hospital.'

'Louise was *anorexic*.' Lee shakes her head. 'She'd had problems for years. Nothing to do with Caro, or anybody else.' She stubs out her cigarette. 'That was ages ago, anyway. Caro's into other stuff now.'

'Yeah,' Martha wades in. 'She's swapped her tarot cards for placards. Caro the activist. Her politics are fake. Like everything else. She just wants everyone to talk about her, like we are now. She doesn't believe in anything except herself.'

That puts a stopper on the conversation.

They go out, leaving me alone in the house. I don't mind. I would have gone out with Cal, but he's otherwise occupied. Also, I'm skint. I've spent all my allowance and my summer job hasn't properly started – like I haven't been paid yet. I clear up in Martha's room and open the window wide. I take the bottles downstairs and put them in the recycling, under a pile of other stuff, so Mum won't notice.

I like having the house to myself. When I was a kid, I used to mooch round and round, going into rooms, poking into drawers, trying to discover the parts of people's lives that they kept secret from me.

Mostly, I was looking for my dad.

He was in the Army. He went out one day on exercise when I was three, wearing a Bergen that was bigger than me, and he never came back. Killed in an incident involving live rounds. An accident. I don't remember much from the time when it happened. I don't remember anything much about him at all. Just that I associate him with the wardrobe, for some strange reason. Mum kept his dress blues in there. After it happened I remember climbing in and seeing the uniform hanging there, all swathed in plastic. Scared the life out of me. I thought it was his ghost. Maybe that's why the wardrobe makes me think of him.

His hat was on top, in a box that I was told never to touch. I used to wonder if that was where his head was kept.

Mum got rid of it all years ago. There's no trace of him in her room now, except for the medals he got in the First Gulf War. She keeps those in her jewellery box.

Rob used to go round the house wearing them. He remembered Dad better than I did. He used to tell me stories about him, about the battles he'd been in, the action he'd seen. I believed every word until I began to watch movies and read books for myself. Rob gave Dad the hero role in every book he'd read and film he'd seen, from Andy McNab to *Black Hawk Down*. That was the first chink in my hero worship. I couldn't figure out why he did it. I was bound to find out sometime or other.

My brother joined up as soon as he was old enough, following in the family tradition. Grandpa, Dad, then Rob. His room hasn't changed that much from when he went off to join his regiment. The walls are still plastered with Army posters, Page 3 totty, Girls Aloud and pictures of different models of guns, broken into parts and assembled. There are photos of him and his mates. He'd pin new ones up every time he came back from a posting. They all look the same wherever they are in the world. A bunch of guys standing about in combats, posing in their Wiley-X shades, holding guns, swathed in rounds, meaning business; either that or they are in a bar on R&R in Cyprus or somewhere, dressed in shorts and T-shirts, or bare-chested, pissed and sweating, red eyes glaring, grinning with arms round each other, clutching a bottle or a glass or a girl. The colour has faded in some of the photos, the corners curled; others have fallen off the wall. I thought Mum would be straight up here with the step-ladder and paper stripper as soon as he moved out, but no. She's left it just as it is. Maybe she secretly hopes he might come back. Fat chance of that.

He lived here for a bit after he was discharged from hospital, but only for a little while. Being at home got on his nerves. He couldn't stand Mum fussing over him. It wasn't his leg and the help he needed with that. It was the nightmares. He'd shout out in the middle of the night, wake up screaming. He didn't want us hearing; it made him look weak, vulnerable, and he didn't like us seeing that. He didn't want Mum going in, trying to soothe him, like he was a little boy again. He used to have nightmares back then, but these were of a different order. In the end, he seemed to give up on sleeping. I'd hear him padding up and down, prowling about the house. The creak on the stairs, the squeak of the laminate when he was trying to be quiet were more disturbing than the shouting.

He couldn't take Mum worrying, talking about therapy. He'd had that and it hadn't done anything. He had his own way of dealing with it, involving the stuff he grows and cans of Carlsberg Special. In the end he moved in with Grandpa where he was freer to do things his own way. Grandpa's deaf as a post and even if he did wake up, he'd say nothing. He understood. He had nightmares of his own.

I grab a beer from the fridge and head out on to the patio. We live on an estate, like lots of others that border the town. The houses are set about in little closes at angles to each other so they all have their bit of private space. A new section gets bolted on every few years. Like Legoland. The estate looks bare, unfinished. This was all fields not that long ago. The trees and hedges that were here before have been replaced by spindly little saplings and shrubs. Mum tries to grow things up the fences and has planted out the borders, but the garden is like a green box. The houses are bright brick, unweathered.

It's a nice night. The barbecues are on the go. It makes me hungry. I go in and fix myself a bacon sandwich. Come back out to eat it. People are in their gardens. I hear the snatches of conversation, the clink of glasses, bursts of laughter.

I stay out for a long time. The lights die all around me, there's just the distant street glow. It's fully dark now. A clear night. The air is still warm and soft as velvet. I look up into the blackness dotted with specks of light. Grandpa had a telescope up in his attic. We used to look at the stars together. I remember the constellations. He taught them to me. I see a shooting star, like a golden pin scratch, then another. I watch out for more, my mind drifting. I see the star tattoo on her shoulder. The pattern of tiny freckles, like constellations. I wonder what her skin would feel like under my fingers. I try to conjure her. I see her profile in close up as she looked over her shoulder; caught in the mirror as she looked from her own reflection to her mother. I re-run those moments again and again, taking in the dark sweep of her brow, the liquid gleam of her eye, the tilt of her nose, the curve of her lip, the shadow under her cheekbone, the fall of her hair. I open my eyes and look up at the sky. A song comes on to my iPod shuffle. I've heard it, even liked it, but the words have never meant that much to me before. Now they do.

6

I've got a summer job down by the river, working for Alan's Boat Hire, collecting the money from deckchairs, selling ice cream, taking boats out. I've been doing it for quite a few summers. I kind of inherited it from Rob. He used to work down here before he joined up. I don't start officially until the holidays but business has been picking up with the good weather and Alan's asked me to do a few evenings after school. It doesn't pay much, Cal takes the piss unmercifully, but it's outdoors and by the river. That's good enough for me.

One afternoon I'm sorting out the punts, jumping from boat to boat, getting them in a neat row, making the poles tidy, checking that they all have their complement of cushions. It's surprising how often those get lobbed into the water. I glance up and that's when I see her. Under the willows with her things spread out around her, writing in a notebook.

I have the feeling that she has spent the day under the trees, hidden by the screening leaves. There's been no sign of her at college and, believe me, I've been looking. I'm so busy staring that I catch my foot and nearly fall in the water. She starts laughing. She's watching me, too. I feel my face heating up and turn away quickly, pretending to be busy.

The next time I look she's up with her bag slung across her shoulder. Her step is as light as a dancer's as she walks across the grass.

'It's Jamie, isn't it? Jamie Maguire? Martha's brother? I saw you in the cafe the other day.'

'Oh, yeah.'

'So let's stop pretending we don't know each other, shall we? Are you for hire?'

'Yeah, sure.'

'How much?'

I nod towards the notice. '£10 for half an hour.'

She takes out a twenty. 'Here. Give me an hour.'

I take the note from her and push it into the money bag I wear round my waist.

'Where do you want to go?'

'As far as you'll take me.' She steps into the boat. 'As far as we can go.'

I help her to a seat and push off. She leans back against the cushions, trailing one hand in the water. She doesn't say anything, so I don't either. She's wearing sunglasses so I can't see her eyes, but I have a feeling that they are closed. I take advantage of the chance that gives me to study her. I turn the boat away from the bridge, where the water gets too deep for punts. I know where I want to take her. I let the pole slip through my fingers using it as a rudder, allowing the flow of the current to take us downstream.

'This is it.' I turn the punt in towards the ait, the first link in a chain of small islands above the weir. 'We have to stop here.'

I jump out and pull the punt in under the willows, securing it to a low branch. I angle the boat into the bank, so she can step straight out without getting her feet wet. I'm standing ankle deep, but wouldn't want her to lose one of her flimsy shoes in the sucking mud. I scramble up on to the bank to help her out. She holds on to my arm and I take her sudden weight. She does not let go as she steps on to the bank.

'What a magical place.'

She reaches out and brushes the brown, furry tightness of a bulrush, then reaches down to touch the waxy, pale green spears, the curling yellow flowers of an iris. I smile. I knew it would have this effect. It's like stepping into a green cave, the walls woven from living willow. She's holding my hand, like she's forgotten to let go of it, and we walk across ground carpeted with thick grasses studded with golden buttercups. On the other side of the island is a pool. The water here is deep and clear. It brims, before spilling over the lip and gushing and tumbling down the steps of the weir.

'Can you swim here?' she asks, peering down past the small, darting fish into the brown depths.

'I suppose you could.' I shrug, although there are notices up prohibiting it. 'It's probably not very clean, though.'

I wrinkle my nose. The weir gives off a faintly chemical smell. At the bottom, the churning of the water is throwing up foam from detergent dissolved in the water.

'Can you get across here any other way?'

'There's a wooden bridge, leads over from the old allotments. It's pretty rickety and taped off. Part of it was swept away in last year's floods.'

'What's over there?' she asks, pointing across the weir.

'Nothing much. It's like this, only smaller. They're called aits. Little islands in the river. You can't get to that one from the land. You have to cross the weir and the stones are slippery.'

'What would happen if you did slip?'

I look over the weir at the ribbed concrete steps, the thick, hissing rush of the tumbling water, the turning churn at the bottom of the race.

'You'd probably drown.'

'I want to go over there.'

She's let go of my hand and is taking off her shoes. She sets off, striding across, as sure-footed as a water bird.

'Watch out for the one in the middle!' I shout, but she's already stepped over that, as if she knew to avoid it.

I start after her. The soles of my trainers slip on the stones. I'd have been better off in bare feet but it's too late for that now. A couple of slabs in the middle are loose and get pushed out of place by the winter spates. They rock and wobble under my heavier step, threatening to tip me over into the racing water.

We used to cross the weir for a dare when we were kids. We'd bike down here or come over from the allotments. Grandpa and Rob would do proper fishing with a rod; I'd rummage about with a net for taddies and tiddlers and put them in a jam jar. I used to get upset when they took my catch to use as bait. Later, Grandpa bought me my own rod and Rob and I used to go over to the island. Rob reckoned there were pike in the reeds where the river was deeper. I never liked crossing the weir. He'd flit over, light-footed and sure of his balance, being afraid is not in his nature. I'd get to the middle and wobble. Just like now. It always got me. The rocking would send my legs rigid. I don't like heights and I don't like walking on ledges. I don't like that feeling of being balanced between things. I always think that I will fall and it won't be pleasant whichever way I go.

'Don't look!' she shouts from the other bank. 'Don't stop. Just keep going!'

This time she's the one holding out a helping hand as I throw myself on to the bank.

'It's even better here,' she says.

The willows are thicker. There are people on the river bank, boats out, but it's as though we are alone in the quiet green cage of our own world. Fallen willow leaves make a soft, silvery carpet. I show her where we used to build fires and try to cook things, like we were in some kids' book. There was a pile of those in Grandpa's shed. He used to bring them for us to read when it was raining. He'd buy them off the second-hand stall in the market. They are still there in the corner, covered in spider's webs, pages as thick as blotting paper, puffed with damp: *Swallows and Amazons*, *Famous Five* – books about kids who had adventures and their very own islands. This was *our* island. We felt like them.

'I like it,' she says. She drops her voice to a husky whisper. I feel her breath on my neck as she speaks close to my ear. 'I like the way that people can't see us, even though they are really near.'

I can hear voices talking on the river walk, a warning shout from the river and laughing as oars splash and a boat turns back from the weir. There's something in her face. Something in the way she smiles. The way she looks at me. An invitation. She's excited by the proximity of other people. She moves closer. I should kiss her. Put my arms round her. Push her down on to the rough counterpane of leaves. That's what Rob would do. He used to bring girls here when he worked the boats.

I don't do any of that.

'We'd better be getting back,' I say. 'The hour's almost over.'

On our way back, we pass the old allotments. I look up automatically, to see if Grandpa is there, to give him a wave. He's not, of course. He's not allowed out on his own any more. Someone's been working his plot, though. The shed's undergone some running repairs, too. Rob must have been down doing some work for him in between tending his own plantations. He wouldn't want Grandpa thrown off for not maintaining the plot. He'll never come back here, but Rob likes to keep up the fiction. Rob can't stand to think that the old man has changed for ever. Besides, he doesn't want someone else taking over his garden. That would interfere in his operations.

Grandpa's shed is substantial, more like a little chalet. Years ago, people used to come down here in the summer to be by the river and out of the town. They were like holiday homes. There aren't many left like that now.

'One of them belongs to my grandpa,' I say.

'They're cute.' She looks over her glasses. 'Like summer houses or something. Can we take a look?'

I shrug OK and steer the punt into a little landing stage and tie up. We walk up through the allotments. I go first, stamping down grass, pushing brambles out of the way. It's a bit wild down here. Some of the allotments aren't kept up. Down by the river, they tend to flood. She walks behind me picking raspberries, sucking in the soft warm pulp of the fruit.

I feel for where the key is hidden and unlock the heavy brass padlock. It's warm inside, stuffy. I prop the door to let in some air and let out the signature shed smell: a mix of seed, fertiliser, weedkiller with an undernote: a heady, pungent, bittersweet reek.

She wrinkles her nose. 'Can I smell cannabis?' she asks and smiles.

'Yeah.' I smile back. 'My brother. He uses it as a curing shed. He's got little plantations of it dotted about, hidden in the orchard out back and on plots that aren't worked any more.' Feathery fronds growing up behind corrugated iron enclosures on deserted allotments, tall plants thrusting through the nettles and brambles down by the river. 'He brought the seed back from Afghanistan, last tour but one.'

'Oh, yeah. He's in the Army, right?'

'Used to be. He got invalided out.'

'I heard that. What happened, exactly?'

'He was caught by an IED. Roadside bomb. His leg was pretty smashed up. Reckons he needs the weed for medicinal purposes.'

She nods, taking in the information. Most people express shock, sympathy. She's not most people.

'He's pretty much all right now,' I add, as if she'd asked.

His leg wasn't the only thing that got damaged, but I don't go into that. There's a patch that's been newly worked. The weeds cleared. Freshly dug. That must have been hard for him. I'd have come down to lend a hand. We used to work on the allotment together, helping the old man, but times change. Back then, I was always in the way, doing the wrong thing. Just a nuisance. Now he needs my help but asking is beyond him. That's how it is.

The shed is like a time capsule. There are the books I was thinking about and propped up against the wall is the table tennis table we begged off a bloke who was taking it to the tip. There's a broken settee and a whiskery old wicker chair, the sprung seat covered by a faded cushion. A couple of empty bottles are down by the side of it. A pyramid of cans in the corner. A different kind of recreation. I look out again. The light is changing to the gold of evening.

'Time to go,' I say to her. 'Alan will be sending search parties out soon. He'll think we've gone over the weir. It's the punt he cares about more than us. They're very expensive. Hard to replace.'

I settle her back in the craft and begin poling us back to the boat station. She goes distant on me. I can't tell what is going on behind her shades. We're back to punter and passenger. That moment under the willows might never have happened, it's sliding away like the water under the till.

'I thought I might've seen you around,' I say, shoving the pole into the river. 'At college, I mean. I heard you were transferring.'

'Where did you hear that?' she asks, suddenly alert.

'Oh, um.' I realise my mistake. A little too late. 'Martha. Didn't you used to be friends with her?'

'What makes you think that?'

'You came to one of her birthdays. Don't you remember?'

She doesn't answer, just stares down at the water. The distance between us widens. I try another tack.

'It's just that I was, um, well, you know . . .'

'Making enquiries?'

I thought she might be annoyed to know I'd been asking about her, but she smiles, like she's flattered and, anyway, she's used to people talking about her and isn't bothered.

'Yes.' I grin. 'I guess. Someone said you were moving to ours.'

'That is correct.'

'That's why I thought I'd maybe see you . . .'

'Haven't started yet. Don't intend to go until next term. I might not go at all. I hate schools.'

'Ours is a sixth form college.'

'Same difference.'

'What will you do instead?' I ask. We seem to be steering into safer water. At least she's talking.

'Oh, I don't know . . .'

She stretches out her legs. She's sitting facing me. She wears a thin gold chain on one ankle. In the delicate blue hollow, like the shadow of the bone, there are striations, straight little marks, slightly raised, scored across the white skin, like a bar code. She touches the place as if rubbing an itch activated by my looking.

'I might go travelling,' she says. 'Or go to London, try modelling. Go to Paris. Or Berlin. Get a job there doing anything. I'm pretty good at languages. Pick them up quickly.'

'Don't you want to go to uni?'

That's all the rest of us think about. We never consider other possibilities. She makes us seem like a bunch of sheep.

'Who said I didn't? I just don't want to go *yet* and I don't want to go here. I'd prefer the Sorbonne, or Tübingen.'

'Where's that?'

'Germany.' She looks at me like she wants to add 'stupid'. 'I want to do Politics, but I want to study abroad.'

I don't know anyone who's planning to study abroad. Compared with her, we seem ordinary, unambitious, provincial. She knows about places we've never heard of. I think she's going to ask about what I'm planning to do, my choices of university, like most people, but she doesn't ask me anything. Instead she remarks:

'You're pretty good with that pole.'

'I've had plenty of practice. I've worked down here since I was fourteen. I'm here most nights once the season has started and most days in the holidays.'

We're nearing the station. I tie up and help her out.

'Most nights, eh?' she says as she takes my hand. 'I'll have to remember that. See you again sometime,' she says over her shoulder as she walks away.

Why didn't I say something to detain her? Why didn't I ask her out? Ask for her number?

I watch her go, cursing myself for a fool.

7

Perthro: a secret matter
Elder Futhark – Runic Alphabet

Jamie Maguire. I don't see him for years then it's twice in a few days. The power of coincidence, you could say. The workings of chance. Although chance didn't make me hire him. Chance didn't make me go on a boat ride with him.

I had to pretend I'd never been on the ait, of course. Never crossed the weir. Wasn't that strange the way I knew to look out for the rocking stone? Spooky! As though I really am psychic. I had to pretend that I'd never been to the allotment, that I'd never even seen the cute little chalet, let alone been in it. That I didn't know Rob. I can't mention that. It would make everything too complicated, and I don't like complicated.

And then there's Martha's birthday. What made him bring that up, I wonder? Maybe he's the one who is psychic.

Do I remember? Of course I remember. Martha's fifteenth. I was fourteen. I'm nearly a year younger than her. It's an awkward age for birthdays. Too young to go out properly, too old for jelly and ice cream. We all went out for a pizza, then to the multiplex and back to hers. I remember perfectly, I have an excellent memory, but even if I hadn't, even if I had the memory of a single cell amoeba, I'd remember that night. You always remember the first time, don't you?

8

End of term. The Big Night Out. She's bound to be around. Cal's calling round about eight. He's been let off the leash. He's allowed to go out with me because Sophie is having a night with the girls. I've got plenty of time. I always like the getting ready. Having a shower and a shave, getting my hair right, picking out clothes. There's a fight for the bathroom. Martha is going out, too, and she'll take an age. When I hear the door chimes go, I'm ready. I run down the stairs and out. I'm always away first. Martha will be hours yet.

The day is tipping towards evening, the blue sky darkening, the street lights coming on. It's warm. There are kids out playing on the front lawns and the barbecues are on the go again. We walk quickly. I wave away the half-bottle of vodka that Cal takes from his pocket. I need to keep sharp. I don't want to get wasted in case I run into Caro. He snaps open his tobacco tin and lights up a thin spliff. Definitely kicking out tonight. 'Your brother's home-grown is good stuff.' He squints at me through the smoke.

We cut across the park. Groups of kids are gathering in circles. The ones who are too young to get into the pubs. They are passing round bottles of cider, WKD, Breezers, cans of Carlsberg, anything they've managed to get their hands on. We walk past, chatting about when we used to do that. I had the same feeling then. Excited to be out. Anticipation. The feeling that anything could happen. *This* time, it just might. It might just be the perfect night.

Along the High Street, gangs of girls walk together, strung in lines across the pavements, arms linked, high heels clicking, in a uniform of tight tops, short skirts, bare shoulders, bare legs, bare midriffs spray-tanned the colour of caramel. Boys swagger in tight groups, eyeing the girls and each other. T-shirts, polo shirts, short-sleeved checks, make of jeans, how they are worn, sneakers, basketball boots, trainers, all mean something, mark them as belonging to one tribe or another. The students have all gone home for the summer. It's our town now. Bouncers stand outside the pubs, legs apart, necks bulging, sweating in their black, muttering into their head sets, adjusting their mirror shades.

We are standing outside one of the cool bars. It used to be the Rose and Crown but now it's called MoJo and has a cocktail menu on every table and big squashy sofas, as opposed to one of the vertical drinking sheds that Cal favours, with offers on all the drinks, big screens and loud music and no one looking too closely at the fake ID.

'There's a queue,' Cal objects. 'We'll never get in. There's bound to be a dress code and we're wearing jeans and T-shirts. Anyway, that kind of place, they won't let anyone in underage. Our cards will never fool them.'

The bouncers are a cut above the average. Sharp suits and designer shades. Not fat like most of them, but definitely powerful. There's a woman with them, checking names for the VIP area. Bad sign indeed.

'Yeah, yeah. We'll get in. Just chill.'

I'm by no means certain, but I've just seen Caro go in with that Art teacher guy. So much for that being over. I'm beginning to wonder about Lee as a source of information. The woman with the list waves them in, no problem. I've been on the hunt for her all evening and I'm not about to give up now I've seen her. I drag Cal into the queue.

My confidence wanes the nearer to the front we get. Most of the other people are older than us, and not so casually dressed. The doormen are already assessing with their eyes, looking along the line, deciding who'll get in and who won't make it. I'm pretty sure we come into the latter category. The lady with the list doesn't even look at us. We are beneath her notice. Her smile and her, 'Hi! Nice to see you!' switch on and off automatically, alternating with a snotty, 'Your name's not here. So sorry.'

Cal's getting restive.

'We're wasting valuable drinking time, man!' he says, looking at his watch. 'I said I'd meet Sophie later . . .'

So much for the lads' night out.

'We're near the front,' I say, reluctant to give in and lose face, having to slink off with everyone staring and knowing why, quite apart from losing my chance with Caro, that's if I ever *had* a chance, which when I really think about it, isn't very likely . . .

Cal's phone goes. A message from Sophie. He looks at it, frowning, apprehensive, as if it could bite him, as if she's looking at him straight out of the screen.

'It's Soph.' As if I need telling. 'Gotta go, man.' He peels off from the queue. 'Are you coming, or what?'

I shrug. I don't want to spend the night being ignored by Sophie and her crew. Cal looks at his phone. Another message coming in.

'Gotta go, man!' he says again. 'She's in the King's.' He's off at a trot. 'See you later!'

I'm just about to follow, when I hear, 'Hey, Jimbo! Wait up!'

It's Rob. Nobody else calls me Jimbo. If I object to that, he calls me Jim. I don't like that either, but he doesn't take any notice. 'It's your name, man. What am I supposed to call you?' When I say James, or Jamie, he cracks up laughing and says, 'I'm not calling you that! It'd mean my brother is a poncy middle-class twat.'

He's with his mates. They are marked out as Army by

58

the short hair and the way they are built. They make everyone else look puny, even the guys who work out. Bronzed from their last tour. Biceps bulging, tattoos showing, shirts open and flapping, exposing their rock solid six-packs. Rob's not Army any more but he still has mates in and he drinks with them when they come into town.

'All on your own?'

'Cal's left.' I say. My eyes flick up the line to the bouncers. 'He was worried that we won't get in.'

''Course you will.' Rob pulls me to him, his arm on my shoulder. 'I want to buy a drink for my little brother. You come with me.'

The doormen are ex-Army. One nod and we are in. Just like that. Rob's good-looking and can be charming when he wants to be. His smile is wide and the bullet-graze scar on his cheek dints in like a dimple. The woman with the list is unable to resist that smile and the faraway, pale blue eyes focusing down on her. We're not just in, we're VIP.

There's no one I know, so I stick with Rob and his mates, all the time keeping watch on Caro. She's with the Art teacher guy and his friends. They've got a whole corner, sitting on a horseshoe of sofas round a big table, drinking wine. They are all much older than her. Teachers of the less boring kind. People with jobs in things like design and consultancy. They are talking loud. Fancying themselves. He's perched on the arm of a sofa, like a king talking to his court. He's ignoring her and she looks bored. I'm wondering how to get to her, when Rob gives me a pint.

'Here you go.'

Rob's glass is already two thirds empty. Someone hands him a shot and he downs it with a quick grimace and a shake of the head. His mates keep the rounds coming. Security are sending them over, too. It's not pity. It's recognition of what happened to him. What he was like out in Afghan. He's a bit of a hero.

'Drink it!' he says to me. 'Don't sip it! You'll get behind.' I take a couple of gulps.

He's looking round, eyes never still, assessing: ways in, ways out, who's here: male, female, type, age, dress, distribution about the room. He notices everything. It's like he's still looking for assassins. He's jumpy. Nervous. His good leg won't keep still. The fingers on his left hand drum against his thigh, keeping his own time, faster, more frenetic than the music being played by the DJ. He needs drink to relax and he needs a lot of it. He stops doing the whole room and concentrates on the women. His eyes flick from group to group. Girls on a night out; girls just with a friend sharing a bottle of wine, girls in mixed groups, girls with their boyfriends. He whispers comments in my ear, assessing availability, physical attributes. I have to be careful not to spray my drink everywhere. Definitely funny but not PC.

'There's a lot of posh crumpet in here tonight. Anyone you fancy, young *Jamie*?' He drains his pint. 'I prefer slappers myself. Less trouble.'

He used to have a girlfriend, Sonia, they were going to get engaged, but she dumped him after he came back. So much for tie a yellow ribbon and stand by your man. The experience may have coloured his feelings towards women.

'What about her?' He's pointing at Caro. 'Do you fancy that?'

'Might do.' I take a drink.

'Thought so. You've been eyeballing her non-stop. What are you going to do about it?'

I shrug again.

'If you won't, I will.'

He makes to go over. I catch his arm.

'No, Rob! She's *with* people?'

'So?' He turns to look at me, eyes mixed with pity and puzzlement. 'She is not with *people*. How many times do I have to tell you? She's with a bunch of *arseholes*! There's no point in standing here crying into your pint. You got to strike, little bro, or you won't get any.'

He's gone before I can stop him. I watch as he leans over and whispers something to her. She looks up and smiles. He says something else and she laughs. He jerks his head in my direction and she looks at me. I give a wave, feeling really stupid. I don't know what he's said, but it looks like she might come over. That's when the Art guy gets involved. He steps in front of Caro and squares up. I guess he expects Rob to back down, he's a big guy and Rob's quite a bit shorter, but that is not going to happen. Rob steps up to him, fists closed, arms corded.

His head goes back, just a fraction. I know what he's going to do. My eyes close in sympathetic reflex action. I'm expecting to hear the crunch of cartilage, hear the guttural howl through a throat thick with bubbling blood. But that is not what happens. Caro pushes Rob back with the flat of her hand. She gets the Art guy away. She handles it. It's as if she has guys fighting over her every day.

The friends move with them. The place they left is immediately filled by another group. Rob doesn't come back to me. I lose track of him temporarily as I finish my drink. Bryn, one of his mates, hands me another so I chat to him for a bit.

I've met him before. Him and Rob were in the same platoon. He's Welsh. Tall and dark, deeply tanned from his recent tour. His hair is so short that his scalp shows white under the changing lights; the black bristling cut glistening with sweat and gel. He has calm brown eyes. He looks tough but kind. He's just been made sergeant and I can see why. He was Rob's best mate when he was 'in'. Looked after him. He's a sniper. They all are. He was Rob's Number Two, his spotter, finding targets, checking things like range and wind direction, covering his arse. They worked together, close as brothers. He crosses his arms and I see the sniper's tattoo, a pair of crossed rifles with an 'S' above it, that he has on his upper arm. Rob's is on his thigh.

Bryn's just come back from a tour in Helmund.

When I ask how it was, he just says, 'Hot. Yeah. It was hot there.'

He won't talk to me about it. There's no point because I won't understand. Only they know what it's like to be out there. They have their own language. They talk to each other in special terms and acronyms: L69s, SA80s, sangars, HESCOs and GMGs, VSPs, IEDs and FOBs. He won't talk to me about it unless I ask specific questions and I know not to ask.

He's older than the others. He talks about his leave, coming home to the wife and kids. He couldn't wait, counting down the weeks, then days, then hours, but he's already had enough. He wants to be back there, I can see it in his eyes. He wants to be back in the desert heat, laying up on a roof somewhere under the flutter of a camouflage net, looking down his L69 'long' through his SIMRAD night sights, going out in the LAV, checking things out through his NVGs, or whatever it is they do there. He loves it and hates it. They all do. That's why they get pissed and kick off. Trying to get that adrenalin rush, trying to generate some excitement.

'Your dad was in, wasn't he?' he says to me.

'Yeah, my grandpa, too. We're a military family.'

'Ever think about joining yourself?'

'Nah,' I shake my head. 'It's not for me.'

'What do you want to do, then?' he asks as he buys me another pint.

'Doctor,' I say, although that's not me, that's Martha. I haven't got a clue what I want to do.

'You can be a doctor. They'll pay for your education. Training. Everything.'

'Yeah, I know. But I don't want to.'

I want to add, 'Look what happened to Rob', but I don't. It's not the right thing to say. He picks it up, anyway. The words unspoken.

'Shit happens,' he says quietly. 'I miss him. We all do. He was the best. Top kill tally in the unit. Three tours and hardly a nick. Goes out on routine patrol and boom . . .' He sighed. 'You need eyes in your arse out there. Lose concentration. Just once and . . .' He shook his head. 'Could happen to any of us. How's the boy doing? Seems all right.'

His laugh is a deep rumble in his throat. We look over to where Rob is chatting to some bird.

'Umm,' I take a pull on my pint. 'That's just tonight.'

'Having trouble, is he?' He looks at me, suddenly serious. Soldiers will make a joke out of almost everything but he really cares about Rob. I can see it in his eyes. 'Having a problem settling back in, like?'

I nod. He's guessed right.

'He's best off out of it, you know.'

'That's not how he sees it. He loved it. It was his life.'

'Still best off out of it. It was getting to him. He was getting obsessive. Going out on little ops of his own, settling scores, strictly against orders, of course. It doesn't do to get involved like that. It doesn't do to forget that the target is a human being.'

'He's been talking about going back. Says there are ways, but I didn't think he could. You know, with his leg.'

'He don't mean Army. He could sign up with one of the private outfits.'

'You mean mercenaries?'

He laughs. '"Private Security Services" is what they call them.'

'But what about . . .'

'His injuries? That don't matter. He's got special skills has your brother. All they got to do is get him in and get him out. He just has to hit the target. He don't have to put up with the rest of the bollocks.'

'Do you think he'll really do that?' I wonder how Mum will react.

'Could do,' he shrugs. 'It's an option. I hope he don't, though. Wouldn't be good for him, you know? None of us to watch his back and those people ain't got no scruples. No code, if you know what I mean. Work like that can do damage and there's been enough done already.' He had a look of a man who's said too much and not enough. He stared into his empty pint, as if he was wondering where it had gone. 'You want another?'

'No thanks, I'm good.'

He leaves me to go back to the bar and I'm thinking about going when I feel a heavy arm across my shoulders. It's Rob.

'Where are you off to, little bro? Going after that piece you've had your eye on?'

'No,' I say, although that is what I had in mind.

'Wouldn't bother if I was you. No point.' He shakes his head slowly. 'She's out of your league.'

65

'Maybe.'

'Most certainly.'

I don't know how much he's had, but a lot by the look of it. He's about to turn on me, I can see it in his eyes.

'Seems like she prefers grown-up arseholes, not baby ones, like you.'

He snorts a little bit, as though that's funny, and smiles a special tight smile. He gives me the stare, like there's no one there behind the blue eyes. He's always had a tendency to switch like that. Nice one minute, the next – watch out! He's goading me, gauging the effect his words will have, waiting to see if I'll react. He'll go on until I do.

'I just gotta go. That's all,' I say again. 'There's no one in here I know. I want to go on somewhere else.'

'Where?'

'I don't know. I haven't decided. Wherever it is, you wouldn't like it.'

'Why's that?' His voice is quiet, like he's searching for another way in to me and thinks he's found it.

'It'll be full of kids my age.'

He looks at me for a long moment. The beer's getting to me. I haven't been sharp enough. I have taken a wrong turn.

'You're ashamed of me,' he says.

'No, I'm not!'

I turn away. I don't want to go into this old chip on the shoulder stuff, the resentment he's set up against me and Martha just because we've opted to stay on at school and both plan to go to university when he left as soon as he could. It's been there ever since he got back, but it's worse when he's drunk. It's stupid. Something he's manufactured to get at us. I don't want to think that it could be more than that. Some kind of paranoia.

He grabs hold of my arm to pull me back. Not willing to let go of me or the argument he's conjuring. It's as though he needs it. Feeds off the aggravation.

'Yes, you are. You and Martha. You think I'm a bit of a townie, while you two get more stuck up by the day. At least she's honest about it. Says it to my face. You know what you remind me of? The Ruperts. Useless junior officers called Jonty and Tim and Toby. Pack of wankers. You're just like them. You are a little . . .' he whispers the short, blunt word in my ear, his breath hot, yeasty with beer. 'If you weren't such a little –' he says the word again, louder; people are beginning to stare – 'you'd want me and the lads to come with you. Introduce us to your Rupert mates and their posh-bird girlfriends.'

'It's not like that and you know it. I just want to go. Don't be stupid!'

His grip tightens at the word 'stupid'.

'I told you not to call me that!'

'Leave him go, Rob, mate. That's it.' Bryn is suddenly beside us. He prises Rob's hand off my arm and holds him tight by the shoulders. The other guys are with him.

'Yeah, man,' one of them says, 'let him go and come and have a pint. You're getting behind.'

They close round Rob so he won't kick off. So there won't be trouble. So none of the Security notice.

I rub my arm and head for the door. I'm upset. I hate it when Rob gets that way with me. I'm not really looking where I'm going and the place is crowded now, nowhere to move. I knock into this guy, jogging his pint. The beer spills a bit and he turns on me.

'Oi! Watch it, you little twat!'

He's wearing an England shirt, as are his mates, the dress code has obviously slipped as the evening has progressed.

'What are you doing in here, anyway? Shouldn't you be home with Mummy?' He makes sucking noises, like he's pulling on a bottle. 'Get out of here!' He pushes me into his mates, who push me back towards him. 'There you go again! Smacking into me!'

He gives me another push, harder this time. One of his mates puts a foot out to trip me, send me sprawling. Someone catches me, steadying me up. Then he steps past me.

'Want some, do you? Well, come on then! Have some of this!'

Rob is standing in front of me, fists curled. The guy steps into a fast jab, once, twice, so quick you hardly see it, except there's now blood coming from his nose.

'Anyone else want some?' Rob glares round but the others back away, dragging their bleeding mate with them. 'Thought not.' He turns to me, looking me over, like I'm a little kid again and he's saved me from the bullies. 'You OK? No harm done?'

'I'm fine. I'm OK.'

He drapes his arm round me. Bryn stands back, frowning, eyes assessing, wondering if he's going to hug me or break my neck. But he won't do that. Not now. His anger against me is gone. Dissipated. Transferred to the other bloke.

'You can be a little twat,' he hugs me closer. 'You know that? But you're still my little bro. That girl,' he looks round like maybe she's still here, 'the one you fancy? Go for it. Yeah!' He laughs a little, like it's a joke only he is sharing. 'Why not? She could be good for you!'

He reels off with his mates and I'm left on my own.

It was always like that. He could beat the living shite out of me but if anyone else touched me, they'd better watch out.

I walk along the street thinking about that, trying to find reasons for it. Rob was always unpredictable. When we were kids, he'd be nice and friendly, playing with me, sharing toys, telling stories, then suddenly he'd turn. He'd say things to upset me. Hurt me. Do things to scare me. Lock me in dark places. He'd tell me to climb up into the loft and then take the ladder away. Take me out into the woods, tie me to a tree and then go away and forget about me. Make me eat dirt. He wouldn't stop until I was crying and begging for mercy. The stupid thing was, I'd do it. On occasion, I'd fight back, but it always ended with me getting beat and running home crying.

Sometimes he'd get caught. Martha would tell. Or someone would find me, still tied up with the clothes line, or bruised and sobbing, snot dripping. Mum would want to know why, what on earth happened.

'We were playing a game.' I'd hiccup. 'It was only a game.' I would never tell and he knew it.

He'd turn back just as quickly. It was as if he liked to see just how far he could push me. When he thought that I'd reached my limit, he'd smile and give me his favourite toy. I'd put up with anything, just for that moment.

Martha was different. He usually left her alone. She was only small but she could do some damage and she'd tell Mum in a blink. Or Grandpa. Then Rob would get in trouble for being mean to her. It wasn't just that she was a girl. She didn't care. That was the difference. She didn't want him to like her. She didn't want to be one of his gang. Martha's dislike of him has slowly crystallised into something that borders on hatred. She thinks he's a psycho. I could never feel like that about him. She says that's because I'm suffering from a co-dependency that borders on Stockholm Syndrome. I tell her to take her AS Psychology and shove it.

I check out a few pubs. Most of my friends have left or gone to a club. There are only two in town and they are both useless but I take a look, anyway. Stand in line again, waste even more money. I'm still kind of hoping that I might find Caro, but there is no sign of her anywhere. I decide to call time on a crap night and go home.

I'm just walking past the town hall, when I see him there, sitting on a bench. Caro is with him. I don't stop to think why she's there. I just know I can't leave him. Not in the state he's in.

'Is he all right?' A man comes over. Fluorescent jacket. Black and white reflective police flashes. He squats down.

'Yes, he's fine. He'll be fine. We'll look after him.'

'If you're sure?'

He's not fine and the copper knows it, but it's chucking out time. He looks up, his eyes questioning, asking permission to leave us. There's shouting at the other end of the street. A girl screams. High, excited. Something going down. The policeman walks away. There's plenty to keep him busy.

Rob leans forward. I think he's going to throw up, but he just gobs a mouthful of blood and mucus. His lip is split. His left eye is puffy and closing. Blood leaks from his nose, dripping on to the ground. Spots of blood, shining like garnets in the street light, begin to form a pool. His blue shirt is torn at the shoulder, the front stained dark. He holds his ribs as if they are hurting. He must have had a kicking. His right hand looks swollen with cuts across the knuckles. He must have got a few in before they got him down.

She looks at me expectantly, like I'll know what to do.

I look about at pavements slippery with vomit, the road

glittery with glass, gutters strewn with kebab boxes spilling strips of discarded salad. I feel helpless.

'It's his leg,' I say. 'He can't run. So, if he gets cornered?' I shrug. 'How come you're with him?'

'I'm not *with* him,' she says carefully. 'I was on my way to the taxi rank and I saw him sitting here. I recognised him from the club and came over to help him. See what I could do.'

'What happened to the guy you were with?'

Her turn to shrug.

'He's the Art teacher guy, right? The one who got the sack?'

'Yes, he is.' She turns to look at me. 'I suppose Martha told you all about that, too.'

She takes a bottle of water and a wad of tissues from her bag. She pours the water over Rob's head and face. The shock of it seems to revive him a little bit. His head snaps back and she uses the tissues to begin to wipe the blood from his nose and mouth. Her touch is gentle but I put my hand up to stop her.

'Careful,' I say. 'State he's in, he might lash out.'

'He seems quiet enough.'

We're talking about him like he's an animal. He sits still, slumped forward again, hands dangling between his knees.

I'm just wondering how to get him to the taxi rank and if any of the cabbies will take him when I hear a shout, the sound of feet running. I'm up with my back to Rob and Caro. I don't like fighting, but I can look after myself.

Rob taught me that much. If it's the same lot still after him, I'm not going to let them get him, not going to let them do him any more damage. If it comes to it, I'll fight for him. He's my brother. They'll have to go through me.

It has to be them. They are strung out across the road, coming in a line, taking their time, strutting, fists curled. The girls with them are bunched together, shouting insults, mostly directed at Caro, and egging their lads on. I think I'm done for, but I stand my ground and just hope none of them are carrying.

They begin to speed up, like predators circling in on an easy kill. There's another shout and running feet. Rob's mates. The mob coming for us take one look and veer off in another direction to find some other kind of trouble. The girls follow them, stumbling on their high heels, still shouting insults, whether at us, or them, isn't clear.

'How you doing, then?' Big Bryn takes hold of Rob's chin and tips his face to the light. 'There's a mess on you, all right.' He turns to me. 'Lost track of him in that bar. He went off after some girl and then we couldn't find him. Looks like he found some fun, like. We'll take care of him now.'

He signals to two of the others, who pick Rob up between them as if he weighs no more than a child.

Bryn goes to the kerb to hail a cab. The first one speeds up when he sees the state Rob's in but the next one slows when Bryn waves a £20 note. They push Rob into the back seat and climb in after him.

I give the cabbie Grandpa's address. The cabbie shrugs. He can hardly speak English and doesn't know where it is.

Bryn swears and beckons to me. 'You'll have to show him. Get in!'

'What about her?'

I don't want to leave Caro but there's no room.

'There's a cab coming,' she says and smiles. 'I'll be fine.'

I get in reluctantly. I'd been hoping to see her home, hoping something good could come out of a pretty rubbish night. The cab pulls out. She waves to me. I wave back, then I realise that she's just hailing a cab.

9

Been asking around, has he? Continuing his enquiries. I'm sure Martha and her little posse will have filled him in on everything, all the scandal about Charlie. Not that I care. She'd like me to, they would all like me to, but the opposite is true: I rather enjoy my notoriety. She will have told him about me being expelled, no doubt. Too good a story to miss out. Then there's the time the Head saw me on the six o'clock news – everyone loves that one.

I went down to the demo on the bus from the university. No one else from school would come with me, so I went on my own. What can I say? It was my best day. As soon as we got to the rallying point, I remember thinking: 'This is what I've been looking for. This is it.'

It began quietly, peacefully. Disappointingly ordinary. The crowd moved slowly, ambling at walking pace, chatting and joking. It got better when the chanting started up and the drumming and whistles blowing. Then it felt like we were all part of something, that we owned the street, the city. It was like a festival, a parade where everyone could take part. A Mardi Gras for the masses.

The shouting up ahead was turning into booing and catcalling, consolidating into the consistent, heavy chant: Shame on You! Shame on You! I began working my way to the front, wanting to see what was happening, find the action. The crowd was closing up, moving in a great surge towards the front line. I could see flashes of police fluorescent jackets, the glint of perspex. The police were advancing, reinforced from behind, pushing with their shields, lashing out with their batons, pulling out individuals, kicking them on the ground.

The violence wasn't all one way. All around me, people were snatching up anything they could lay their hands on: placard poles, plastic cones, metal barriers, and hurling them at the police. Everyone cheered when a policeman went down. His colleagues pulled him back, formed a wedge and launched an even more vicious attack. The crowd was spilling into the square and I was getting pushed forward, nearer and nearer to the thrusting shields and flailing batons, when I felt hands on my shoulders. I struggled under the gripping fingers but we were packed too tight together. I couldn't turn.

'They're sectioning the crowd, closing in from the rear,' a voice said in my ear. 'We've got to get out of here.'

It was Charlie. He'd been on the bus, but I'd lost him

in the crowd. He began to move sideways, pulling me with him, holding his camera high, taking pictures over the heads of the crowd. The chanting turned to shouting and screaming as people realised they'd been caught in a trap. Above us, helicopters were circling and there were guys on the periphery filming the crowd, taking photographs, ready to pick people out.

We dodged down a little side alley, dog-legging round to another part of the square. The crowd was more broken up here. A group had surrounded a police van, spraying it with graffiti, using traffic cones to smash the windows. A boy in a black parka with the hood up, scarf over his face, climbed on top of it and was trying to kick the lights off. The rear doors were swinging open, all kinds of riot gear spilling out. I picked up a helmet. Charlie yelled: 'Put it on!' He took a photograph, so did a news cameraman. I gave him the finger. Someone was filming behind him. That's the footage that got on the news. Sirens were sounding in the distance, getting nearer.

Charlie looked around. 'They'll have this part sealed off soon. Time to go.'

There were running battles with the police now. Small groups, like flash mobs, hoods up, faces covered, were breaking off to take the fight on to other places, scattering like sparks in the wind. There was the sound of glass shattering, glimpses of fire. Charlie ran after one group who were kicking in windows and spraying slogans. I went with him. I was shaking all over, but not from fear.

It was the most exciting thing I've ever experienced. I didn't want it to end. I couldn't wait to do it again.

That's how I met Theo. We travelled back with them to the Dean Street Collective in their beat-up old van. If this was a day for new things, new experiences, then Dean Street was a further revelation. They didn't just talk about the day, what they had done. They talked about what the day meant. *They're activists. Black flag anarchists, anti-capitalists, dedicated to changing society by any means necessary, taking action against a violent, oppressive state.*

I thought about the police with their horses and their batons, charging the crowd down, beating people back, really doing damage. I recognised the truth of what they were saying. I knew they were right.

Everything I knew, everything I thought, everything that I had done, my whole life up until that moment, seemed irrelevant and trivial.

Being suspended from school seemed like a battle honour. It meant I could spend more time at their house on Dean Street. It's a run-down terrace in the south part of town. It was always cold and smelt of damp. There were old mattresses everywhere and most of the furniture had been collected from skips, but I loved it there. It had a kind of grungy glamour. The walls were painted red, black and purple, and decorated with slogans and murals

– agitprop artwork. People would turn up at the house from France, Germany, all over, stay a few days then be replaced by others. Always people there. Always something happening. Ideas being discussed. Music being played. Actions being planned.

I was Theo's pet project. He liked the fact that I was still at school. Young minds are the most powerful, unpolluted by compromise. He's older than the rest of them, even older than Charlie. If they had a leader, he'd be it. He's kind of charismatic and they all listen to him. He says that we have reached the cancer-stage of capitalism. Things are happening all over the world, in every country people are taking to the streets, fighting for what they believe. Peaceful protest is not enough. Violence is an inherent and legitimate part of political struggle. If one sets a car on fire that is a criminal offence. If one sets hundreds of cars on fire that is political action. That's what he says. At first, I didn't know what he was talking about, but he lent me books and I found loads of stuff on the Internet. I didn't want to be just a little schoolgirl. I wanted to be able to discuss things on his terms.

He's spent time in Germany. He was in Berlin when the Wall came down. He said he'd been in contact with RZ, a revolutionary urban guerrilla movement who carried out bomb attacks and hijackings in the Eighties and even into the Nineties. Charlie reckoned he was blagging, but I believed him. It sounded amazing. I wished I'd been there with him, but I wasn't even born.

He told me about the Red Army Faction: Andreas Baader, Gudrun Ensslin, Ulrike Meinhof. He told me about their idealism, their passion, their sacrifice. Their martyrdom. They were acting before their time, he said, that's why they were defeated. All the while he was talking, I could feel the hairs on the back of my neck rising. He gave me a badge he'd picked up in Berlin. RAF for Red Army Faction – Kalashnikov and red star. More than that, he was giving me something to believe in. The badge in my hand felt like a talisman. He said it was time for another generation to take up the cause. I'd never felt such a powerful emotion. I went from believing in nothing very much to complete commitment. I guess that's how it is with me. Zero to ten in one go.

The Red Army Faction. I've got their pictures on my wall. Their words in my head. Petra Schelm was the first to be martyred. She drove her BMW through a police road block and was killed by a single shot to the head. She was young, like me. Just twenty years old. When I had my hair cut, Theo said that I even looked a bit like her. I wished that I could have been there, could have known them. It was like falling in love with ghosts.

I would like to do something that is worthy of them. Dedicate that action to their memory.

Theo's moved on, it doesn't do to stay in one place for long, but we keep in touch through chat rooms. Anonymous and totally innocuous. He is part of an underground group. Aktion 262. They are very secret and membership is strictly limited. To belong, you have to prove yourself.

I have a plan but I need an instrument. I might just have found it.

10

'Where did you get to last night?'

Martha's in the kitchen, sitting at the breakfast counter, eating yoghurt and muesli with bits of fruit cut up in it. It looks disgusting, like sick. She's still in her dressing gown but she's probably been up for hours. She's got the sections of the *Guardian* spread out in front of her. She actually reads it, cover to cover, apart from the sport, of course. I think she's a pretentious cow and she thinks I'm a moron because that's the only bit I look at. I go to the bread bin and get out two slices.

'I'm making toast. Want some?'

She shakes her head. 'And don't start frying bacon while I'm in here,' she says without looking up from the paper.

Martha is veggie, has been since she was a little girl and Rob told her where lamb chops came from on a trip to Wales.

'You don't have to worry. There isn't any.' I shut the fridge door. 'Where's Mum?'

'Gone to the supermarket. Hence, no bacon.'

'Is there any coffee?'

'Coffee's bad for you.' She dunks the bag in her herb tea. Caffeine. That's another of her things. 'What happened to your arm?'

I glance down. There's a bracelet of bruises where Rob had hold of me last night. I rub at it, as if it's ink and will wipe away.

I look vague and shrug, as if I can't remember, hoping that Martha won't guess, or question me further.

I put the bread in the toaster and boil the kettle to make the coffee. I drink it black with plenty of sugar.

'You shouldn't have that, either,' she says as I stir.

I take a sip. It's scalding. 'When I want dietary advice, I'll know where to come.'

'Where did you get to last night? I saw Cal with Sophie. Did he run out on you? Leave you all on your own?'

'Rob was out with the lads. I went with them.'

'That must have been fun Alpha male stuff. Let's see how much beer we can throw down our necks, then fight, fuck, curry and spew, not necessarily in that order.'

'Fight is right. I found him outside the town hall. He'd been beaten up. He's OK, thanks for asking. Lads looked after him. Don't tell Mum. She'll only worry.'

Martha shrugs and goes back to the Review. 'Oh.' She looks up again. 'Before I forget. You've got a fan.'

My heart skips. Can she mean Caro? Can't be. If they met, they'd be bound to blank each other. I'm thinking this, but still it could be. They could have bumped into one another. In the Ladies, say, redoing their make-up. Caro could have leaned over, asked to borrow a mascara, and said, 'You know your brother? I think he's really hot.'

'Lee. She likes you.'

I fiddle with the toaster controls to hide my disappointment.

'She's really, really nice,' Martha goes on. 'And attractive. Want me to put in a word? You could do a lot worse. Let me rephrase that slightly. *You* could do a lot worse. Oh, let me think, you *have* done a lot worse.'

''S OK. I'm good at the moment. Want to stay single.'

She looks up. 'And why's that? Because of your burgeoning social life? Without Cal, you *have* no social life. Now him and Sophie are a "couple".' She sketches quotation marks. 'Where does that leave you, Billy-No-Mates?'

'I'm doing all right. If I want your match-making skills, I'll ask.'

'Or maybe you're saving yourself.' Her eyes light up. She's on to it. You can't get much past her. 'That's it, isn't it? You're saving yourself for the divine Caro!'

'Don't be stupid. I don't even know her.'

'But you'd like to, wouldn't you? You'd like to know her really well. I knew it! You're blushing!' She holds up her hands pretending to warm herself. 'No need to use the toaster!'

85

This could go on all morning, but just then Mum comes struggling in through the back door, carting Sainsbury's bags, Jack behind her. 'Hello, you two,' she says. I get up to help her put things away. Martha finishes her muesli.

'Good night?' Mum asks.

'Yeah,' I say. 'All right.'

'Rob got into a fight,' Martha says as she puts her bowl in the dishwasher.

Mum freezes, her hand halfway into the fridge. Her expression changes from sunny Saturday morning to anxious. Any mention of Rob puts years on her. Unless it's good news and it's usually not good news.

She leaves the fridge door swinging open and comes to the counter. Jack takes over putting stuff away.

'Is he all right? How do you know? The police. The hospital. Did they call?'

It has happened before. Sometimes the call doesn't come until Saturday morning. Friday night being just too busy.

'No, Jamie found him bleeding all over the pavement outside the town hall.'

Mum turns to me, her brow furrowed. 'What happened? Is he all right?'

'Yes, he's fine. He'd been in a bit of a fight. The lads took him back to Grandpa's.'

'Why don't you go and see if he's OK?' She says this in a bright and breezy, what-a-good-idea kind of way.

'Do I have to? It's not exactly what I had planned and I'm working this afternoon!'

I've had enough of Rob for the time being. I'm feeling bruised from the night before, and not just on my arm.

'Please, Jamie. It'll put my mind at rest and you know I can't go.'

'Oh, OK.' I figure she's got enough on her plate without me making her life more difficult. Besides, I'm spent up from last night and need to be in her good books.

'You can take him these.' She hands me a stack of ready-meals. 'I'm worried he's not eating properly.'

'And those are "eating properly"?' Martha raises an eyebrow.

'It's better than chips and takeaways.'

'Only marginally.'

'Give it a rest, Martha.' Mum gives her a look. 'I don't want a lecture on nutrition from you.'

Martha doesn't reply but looks mutinous and sulky. Nobody's saying it, but Mum's main worry about Rob isn't to do with food, it's to do with a drug intake and alcohol consumption which is verging on heroic. Mum doesn't know the half of it, but what she does know about has her worried. She'd never blame him for it. He holds such rage deep inside him; drinking and smoking dope are the only way to damp it down. Mum knows that as well as I do.

'Your dad had his own demons,' is what she says. 'I'm the last one to judge.'

It was her forgiveness, her understanding that made it so Rob couldn't stand to be near her. It's better now he doesn't live here, but he doesn't like her going down there. When she does go to see him, she does things that really annoy him, like collecting all the bottles and putting them into the recycling. She doesn't mean to, but she just gets on his nerves.

'Anything else you want me to take?'

'Yes – I've got some stuff in the freezer. I suppose he was drinking last night?'

It's so obvious, I don't even answer.

'He really shouldn't, not with all the medication he's taking.'

'*Supposed* to be taking,' Martha says. 'He knows that, Mum. *We* know that. How do you stop him?'

'That's why I wish he was back here . . .'

Mum stops what she's doing and leans on the kitchen counter. All her concerns about him settling on her, pulling her face down into sagging lines.

'Oh!' Martha turns on her. 'And that worked, didn't it? He still drank like a fish, smoked all the time, came in at all hours, making the whole place stink of beer and take-aways. He never took a bit of notice of you, or any of us. It was a nightmare, Mum, and you know it. It's been loads better since he went down to Grandpa's.'

Mum does not reply. She just winces as though each one of Martha's words is a little tiny blow and goes to get things out of the freezer.

88

'Take these down, too,' she says to me. 'They're home-made.' She looks over at Martha. 'And I wish one of you at least would go and visit Grandpa. He does so like to see you.'

Mum is trying to deflect the conversation away from Rob, but Martha's not having any.

'Never mind Grandpa. He doesn't even know who we are! Rob's a fuck-up, Mum. Why don't you admit it?'

Swearing was a mistake. Mum rallies. 'I won't have you swearing, Martha.'

'Why not? Rob does, so does Jamie.'

'Hey! Don't drag me into it!'

'I don't like *any* of you swearing. Not in the house. You know that.'

'I wasn't swearing as such, Mother, just making a statement of fact.' When she's in the wrong, when she's cornered, Martha shows her claws. 'Perhaps you prefer the term "nutter". Is that more acceptable?'

'He's your *brother*, Martha. I would expect you to be more understanding.'

'Whatever. He's only happy when he's causing trouble, I know that. He's doing it now and he isn't even here. He nearly split you and Jack up and . . .'

'Don't drag me into it, either,' Jack says, trying to make light of it but his shoulders tighten. He carries on putting cans and groceries away.

'I'll be off now,' he says. 'See you later.'

He goes without anyone really noticing. He doesn't

like it when we row like this. Who would? It doesn't happen all that often, and it's always about Rob. Martha's right. He doesn't have to *be* there – he can detonate rows by remote control.

'He's had his problems, you know that, Martha,' Mum says. 'He was very badly wounded. It takes a long time to get over it. It's up to us to be understanding. He's suffering from post-traumatic stress disorder.'

'Is he crap! That's just an excuse for doing what he likes and being a total prick. No one asked him to join the Army. No one asked the Army to go to Iraq and Afghanistan. He joined up because he wanted to. He loved it. He actually *liked* killing people. He told me.'

'You are making out he's a monster.' Mum rounds on her. 'I won't have it.'

'He didn't actually say that,' I point out. 'He said he liked being a sniper.'

'And what do snipers do? They kill people!'

'Only bad guys.'

'We all know that's not strictly true.' Martha glares, defiant, but I can tell that she knows she has gone too far.

The kitchen goes quiet. You can hear the tap drip, drip, dripping in the silence. When Rob first came back, he'd wake up sobbing and Mum would go in to him. He talked to her about things he'd done that he shouldn't. One time, Martha overheard them. She's stored it away to use against him.

'We don't talk about that, Martha.' Mum's voice drops

to just above a whisper. 'Not ever. Do you understand me?'

Martha nods. Her face is still flushed with anger but she doesn't say anything. She bites down on her lip and looks away from me quickly to hide the tears starting in her eyes. However hard she tries to be, she doesn't like to fight with Mum. Mum doesn't like to fight, either. I dash upstairs to grab a shower. I'm still in T-shirt and boxers. I don't want to be around for the hugging and crying and girly heart-to-heart.

11

I go down on my bike. All the curtains are drawn. He's generally an early riser, but after last night I'm not sure that he's going to be up. The door's on the latch, he must have forgotten to lock it last night, so I let myself in. I go into the kitchen to drop off the stuff and he's there, sitting in his boxers, laptop open on the counter. One eye is closed, the lid red and shiny, the skin underneath stained purple shading to black. His nose is swollen, thickened across the bridge, and his lip is cut and puffy. His knuckles are scabbing over. There are bruises as big as hand-spans down the sides of his torso, blue and green circles with purple centres where the boots connected.

'You're lucky your ribs aren't bust.'

I lay the boxes on the counter. The laptop goes to the screensaver downloaded from *The Sun*. He was probably on some porn site. The screen he was viewing comes back momentarily. He wasn't looking at porn; he was looking at guns.

'Will you look at that?' He keeps his finger on the touch pad. 'The Barrett M107 50 cal. Most powerful sniper rifle to date. The bullets are five inches long.' He stretches thumb and forefinger. 'Big as your dick, little brother. It's accurate up to one and a half miles, maybe two. It can punch through concrete, armour-plating. If you get hit by that, you don't get up.'

He closes the site and the screensaver comes back again.

'How's your lip?'

'It's nothing.' He's speaking with a lisp out of the left side of his mouth. 'Must have got hit by a south paw. Don't hurt. Much.' He gives a lopsided grin and his laugh turns to a wince. 'That does.' He reaches across and opens the bag that I've put on the counter. 'Not more stuff from Mum. *Be Good to Yourself*? Jesus Christ! I bet that's Martha.' He squints at it through his good eye. 'Do us a favour and chuck it in the bin.'

But I don't do that. I put it in the freezer. There is no food in the fridge. The shelves are stacked with cans and bottles: Guinness, Murphy's, Stella, Carlsberg, Budweiser, Miller, Magners, all arranged by size and label.

'Stop fussing around.' He reaches past me to take out a Bud, then readjusts a Carlsberg that has got slightly out of line. 'You're as bad as the old dear.'

He pulls the tab and gulps the contents, the beer spilling down his chin and dripping on to his chest. He wipes it round, like it's some kind of lotion.

'That's better!' He lets out a belch. 'Beer's the best thing for a hangover, you know that? What you doing now? I fancy a full English. They do a good one down at Kelley's. Wash it down with a pint of Murphy's. Coming?'

'Nah. I'm on my way to work.'

'Punting the punters, eh?'

'I'm the punter, to be strictly accurate.'

'You said it!' His laugh ends in a grimace. 'Piss off, will you? You're killing me! Literally!' He doubles up. 'They really did my ribs over. Jesus Christ! I think I've punctured something.'

'Sure you don't want to go down the hospital? Check it out?'

'Fuck that! I hate hospitals. Look what they did to Grandpa.'

'He had a stroke. There was nothing they *could* do.'

'That's their story. He was OK when he went in. Next thing you know, he can't find his own arse.'

That's not how it was, but there's no point arguing. Rob loved Grandpa and doesn't like what's happened to him.

'If it gets any worse, I'll get Bryn to strap it for me. It's only what they'd do, anyway.'

'He still here?'

'Yeah, sleeping on the sofa. Couldn't face the wifey

giving him grief. Lads stayed, had a bit of a session. What happened to you? I can't remember that much . . .'

'Bryn gave the cabbie money to take me on home.'

I look through the glass door to the living room. A couple of the guys are in there, sleeping on cushions. A faint reek seeps out: beer and cigarette smoke. All the bottles and cans have been removed and the ashtrays emptied. The magazines on the table are in a squared stack, spines facing out, even if they are porn. Even though his life is in chaos, Rob likes things to be neat. When he lived at home, he'd put his toiletries out in a row on the bathroom windowsill; he even had creases in his flannel. Everything had to be just so; he'd go spare if anyone so much as nudged his razor so it lay at a different angle. Martha thinks he's got OCD – obsessive–compulsive disorder. Mum put it down to wanting to be tidy.

It suited him living with Grandpa. He was the same way. It's probably something to do with being in the Army. Grandpa's stuff is still about the place. His clock is on the mantelpiece, stopped on the day he left the house. Rob won't wind it. Or perhaps he can't be bothered. Grandpa's souvenirs are arranged on the shelf above the telly with his books on military history. Rob keeps them dusted and polished, along with some of Gran's ornaments: a pair of pottery dogs, a shepherd and shepherdess, little china baskets where she used to keep sweets for us. Grandpa only kept a few of her things, enough to remember her by. What Mum didn't want, he sent to Oxfam.

Strange to think that they are all still here and he's not coming back.

'I better get going.'

'Yeah? Say "hi" to Alan for me. Sure you don't want a beer?'

'Nah, I'm good.'

'Please yourself.'

He goes to the fridge to get another can. He looks vulnerable, dressed just in boxer shorts, his nakedness brutally revealing. He's got a lot of tattooings, varying from unrecognisable squiggles to regimental insignia and more elaborate designs that aren't finished, as if he got bored halfway through, or came to and left the tattooing parlour, but it's not the gallery on his arms and chest which attracts the eye. His right leg is quite a bit shorter than the left. He wears an insert in his shoe, so normally it's almost undetectable, but barefoot it's obvious. It gives him a rolling gait, the limp very pronounced. He goes back to the counter and lights a cigarette, stretching out the bad leg. It still hurts him. Aches all the time. The crossed rifles, the snipers' insignia, are high on the thigh. Below that the scars show in silver-white lines, up and down like zips. The muscles are twisted, puckered and pitted where the pins went in, the skin ridged and patched with transplanted flesh. I've seen him rage and cry with frustration, but through all the months of treatment he never complained about the pain. He just endured it. He's brave – no doubt. But the other stuff, the stuff he wants to do but can't, never will be able to, that's getting to him now. I want to help, but there's nothing I can do.

I don't know what to do about him, or the sadness I'm feeling, so I just say, 'See you,' and I go down the hall past Grandpa's photographs of past wars. Him and his mates perched on tanks and armoured cars, grinning at the camera, arms round each other, fags dangling. The photos are faded; all the young men in them are old now, dead or gaga.

'Yeah, see you, bro.'

I leave him staring at his laptop, sucking on a can of beer, his other hand moving as he brings the picture back again. He looks vulnerable. Lonely. His life is fucked and he's going nowhere, living in an old man's house, surrounded by an old man's stuff, in a geriatric cul-de-sac. He hasn't adapted well to civilian life. He hasn't adapted at all. He's stopped going to counselling. He refuses to take advantage of any kind of rehabilitation package. 'Lots of lads got it worse than me,' that's what he says.

He spends his time staring at weapon sites, wishing for his old life, wanting to be looking through his Schmidt and Bender standard sight, targeting the bad man, getting the cross hairs on the Taliban. He's only happy when he's hanging out with his mates, but there's a space between him and them now. Soon, they will be leaving, going back to a life he can no longer share.

I turn away quickly. I wouldn't want him to see me looking. It feels like spying. He wouldn't want me to see him that way. From down the long hall, he's just a dark shape receding, sitting motionless, silhouetted against the strong sunlight like a man in a photograph. His face is as familiar as my own in the mirror, but he looks like someone I no longer know.

12

Jimbo was here just now peeking at what I was doing – you do – don't you, when someone has a laptop open in front of them. Can't help it – human nature. He's thinking I'm looking at porn. That's what soldiers do, right?

But it's not what I'm looking at – I'm looking at the Barrett. I'm thinking what it would be like to use it – to be up on a ridge sighting on something a mile or more away in the rocks and sand and little scrubby trees covered in dust, everything milky brown or shades of grey – with the dust and the wind blowing gritty in your mouth and in your eyes. Always the wind blowing – sometimes hard – sometimes soft – have to compensate for that. Sighting in the cross hairs – hearing the sound of my breathing, then the loading and the shot booming even through the ear defenders – sending birds scattering up into the sky so he looks up to see why and in that beat of a second the bullet rips right through him – pieces of him flying everywhere. He's blown right off the ridge like a suit of clothes. Then the echoes are bouncing off the mountains further and further – growing smaller and smaller until there's only the wind again and me lying still – part of the landscape – wrapped in a sniper smock sprayed to look like the terrain – stuck with dust and sand and dead twigs and branches that rattle as you move into position like a ghost in a ghostly land. No moving around – just hours and hours of keeping still and waiting – then POW!

Yeah that's what I'm thinking about. I'm a sniper – that's what I do.

Sniping is a special thing. You have to be a good shot – that's a given – and it's not like you can't see the target – can't see his eyes and that. You can. Sights you got now – you can see his acne scars. You watch 'em so long you get to know 'em – but you have to be able to separate yourself off – not think of him as another human being. He's the target – that's it – tough shit. It's like hunting – you have to enjoy the tracking and the killing – but I don't think that you are supposed to enjoy it quite as much as I do.

Best thing is when the target don't know you are there – one minute him and his mates are milling about their camp brewing up chai and he's standing there with his AK in his mitt – the next the side of his head goes fitzz in a cloud of red mist. He don't even have time to look surprised and the others haven't got a clue. The shot is echoing all around – or you've used a silencer so no one knows where the fuck the fire is coming from – and they all start running about and as they do you drop another one and another and they're going down like puppets with their strings cut before they can find any kind of cover.

I love it when that happens.

That's not always how it goes of course. It can go the other way. Sometimes the operation goes to shit.

The bad guys have got some useful kit.

You could be set up in a position and the guy right next to you gets blown away by one of theirs with a Russian Dragunov. Or could be you get caught in the open. Nothing you can do as the steel core bullet rips right through the helmet and takes off the top of the skull and half his face with it so it's no longer Lt Johnny Boy Williams I'm looking at just a mess of blood and white chunks of bone. We're on patrol – a hearts and minds mission. He's been showing me pix of his girlfriend on his phone – she's hot. I look up to the compound we're supposed to visit. There's an old doris chucking out water and kids playing and goats wandering about. Seems safe enough. We get out and suddenly there's no one about. Even the goats have buggered off. Johnny Boy is still grinning – thinking about his girlfriend no doubt – and there's a crack like wood snapping and he's thrown back and away from me.

Could've been you. That's all I'm thinking to myself, cos it's not him any more, is it. And I'm glad it's not me. So glad. I drop down on one knee. He was a good lad and a good mate not like the other Ruperts. The interpreter ain't got out of the Land Rover – he's lying flat in the back. I don't blame him for that. Silly fucker who slotted Johhny bobs up to see if he's done damage – so I get him right enough, then another has a look – they are so fucking stupid. I get him, too.

I figure there's a nest of them in there and I leave Johnny where he's fallen. No help for him now and I'm charging up the hill towards their mud shithole of a compound and it's like I'm Kevlar-coated. I can hear bullets zipping all around me – see them kicking up the red dust and splintering rocks – but I keep firing. I kill every fucker in there because they knew.

It's quiet now. I go back to Johnny and wait until Bryn and the rest of them find us. Bryn goes up to the compound. When he comes back he says nothing at all but calls in a strike and it all don't matter because next minute a Spectre gunship flies over and none of them are there any more. There's just a big ball of flame billowing out and nothing left but a black hole in the ground. But when I sleep they are alive again – the old man in the corner and the women with their faces covered whimpering and the little Taliban snappers with their soft sad eyes looking.

I don't sleep very often. We don't talk about that – never talk about that. Sleep like a baby, me. That's what we say to each other. Nothing about what we see when we close our eyes at night. Bryn knows though – he knows what I see because he was there.

Him and the lads are still here but they will soon be going. I don't want them to go. When they're here – it's like there's a barrier between me and what I fear. Don't get me wrong – I don't fear no one. Nothing outside me. What's frightening is what's inside myself – that's why I want them to stay. But then part of me can't wait to see them going out the door so I'm left on my own again – cos that's the only way to be.

Bryn says that I need treatment – to go back and get help. Joking like – always joking – we are always joking – but I know he's serious. Been there done that I tell him – and it's no help because there is no help.

You can't be with your family no more – they just get on your nerves. No matter how much you want to be home, when you're there everyone drives you mental. They don't understand – can never understand. People become unreal – life becomes unreal. The only answer is to go back and be with your mates cos they're the only ones who can understand you. But if there's no going back there's nowhere to go and you don't even want to be with them any more – you don't want to be with anyone. It'll take more than counselling to stop me from going where I'm heading.

13

'This fascist state means to kill us all!
We must organise resistance. Violence is
the only way to answer violence.'
Gudrun Ensslin

I took his phone. It was lying on the bench between us.
He was pretty much out of it and it must have fallen from
his pocket. I could have given it to his brother, but I
didn't. I put it into my bag.

That was careless, leaving it on a bench like that
where anyone might find it. You can tell a lot about a
person from his or her phone: what apps are there, photo-
graphs, texts sent and received, whose numbers they
have in the directory, favourites, websites they access,
emails, depending on what kind of phone it is, even
what kind of tariff someone is on, all these things are
very revealing, the photographs and video footage espe-
cially. A mobile phone is personal, your life in a capsule.
You should look after it. He hasn't even locked it and it
isn't password-protected which is unforgivably sloppy
of him. I look at the photos he's got. The video clips.

Interesting stuff. He's a killer. They all are. I transfer what I want on to my laptop.

The only phone I'll own now is a cheap pay-as-you-go. No numbers. They are in my head. No photographs. I delete every message that I send or receive.

I hadn't seen Charlie for a while. He tells me that getting sacked was the best thing that could have happened to him. Made him focus on his art. Now he's a Real Artist, not just a part-time teacher, and he's doing well. Beginning to sell. He suggests we go back to his place, so he can show me the work he's been doing. That's what he says but I can tell from the way he's looking at me that there will be more to it. I go along anyway. He's got a new flat. A loft space in a converted granary.

He shows me the studio, the work he is doing now. It's very political. Photographs from the London demonstrations merge with images from other countries, burnt-out tanks and buildings, car bombings in Iraq, Afghanistan. The Palestinian flag, the Star of David and the Stars and Stripes merge into one another, torn, blackened and scorched. One huge canvas shows soldiers, their faces erased, bleeding into a reddened landscape, surrounded by scenes of dereliction and devastation. A closer look shows a row of burnt out high street shops; British fields turned into barren no-man's-land, a dead waste ground ribboned with black seeping oil.

'That's oil. See?'

'Yeah. I get that.' I nod slowly, walking up to the canvas and stepping back again, in a suitably admiring way. 'Powerful stuff.'

He grins, arms crossed. Pleased with the effect his work is having, my response.

'I want to show what's happening in the world and what's happening here. Fuse the two together. Literally bring it home to people. What we are doing in Afghanistan, Iraq, Gaza – the Intifada – the destruction and violence we are causing.'

That's enough preliminaries. He pours some wine and we take it through to the bedroom. Maybe he's drunk too much, but it takes him a long, long time. I drift off, and I'm thinking about my appointment with Armani guy. I tell him I want to study Politics. Not here, abroad some-where. I've opted for History, Economics, French and German. 'Can you do it in a year?' he enquires, fingers steepled, head on one side, looking doubtful. 'Your previous subjects were Art, English and Drama.' Mother looks impatient, like my new choices are just a fad. What does she care? If I fail everything, she'd be glad.

'Of course I can,' I say and go on to tell him exactly why. He taps a few notes into his Mac but he's not really listening. He sits back, manicured fingers steepled again.

'By opting for us, you've made a wise choice. We now have Academy status and will soon have a splendid new sixth form and community college, the best in the area. Let me give you the virtual tour of the facilities . . .'

He turns his Mac round and starts a promo video of what it's going to be like. The virtual tour sweeps up to the new Academy buildings off to the right, all smoked glass and wood cladding. The sixth form college will occupy a space on the other side of the drive, so the school reaches almost to the main road. The school is on a rise. The grand front entrance is up a flight of steps (ramp to the side), all glass and chrome. Impressive. Over his shoulder, out of the window, it appears to be a building site. He sees me staring.

'It will be finished by the end of the summer,' he says, reassuring. 'Ready for the opening ceremony on the first day of term. We are expecting a very important visitor . . .'

He mentions a name and sits back in his chair with this self-satisfied look, like we are supposed to be impressed. It'd take more than that, I think to myself and smile. I can hear the chants, like a chorus in my head: Shame on You, Shame on You, Liar, Liar, Out, Out, Out . . .

That's when I have the idea.

It's like a vision, wonderful in its purity. It's a gift. I play it in my head and want to laugh out loud.

Fantasy? Maybe. But I can see a way to make it a reality.

Charlie always falls asleep directly after and I'm as far from sleep as it is possible to be without chemical

110

assistance. I never sleep in the same bed as someone else, that's too high a level of intimacy for me, so I leave him and walk back through town. It's after midnight. I quite like it at this hour. I like the sense of dislocation. The difference between daytime and now.

The traffic lights turn from red to amber to green and back again, but apart from the occasional taxi, there is no traffic to stop. The pedestrian alert sounds out and the green walking sign flashes, although there are no pedestrians as such, just gangs of lads and girls walking up and down the middle of the road, laughing, shouting, talking loud, carrying on some kind of running argument that will probably develop into a fight.

'Who you lookin' at?' a girl shouts at me from across the street, her mouth slack, her eyes black holes inside her sooty make-up. She's big. One strap of the skimpy top she's wearing hangs down showing her breast bulging out of her black bra. The rest has ridden up during the long night exposing rolls of flab, livid white in the orange street lights.

'You. You fat bitch!'

I want to yell, but I don't answer, just shrug and stare back. They don't frighten me. This could be seen as a provocation, but they always back down. Boys don't interfere. They don't fight girls and the girls confine their fights to people they know.

I see him sitting on the bench in front of the town hall. We haven't seen each other for a while but he isn't really in a fit state for a catch up. His speech is more or less incoherent and every time he opens his mouth he looks like he might throw up. I'm no Florence Nightingale. I don't do puke and I'm not terrific on blood and drool so I'm glad when his brother shows up.

Good thing I didn't leave him, though, or I would never have found his phone.

It is like the lock on a safe, as though I'm turning the dial for the right combination and the first tumbler falls into place.

Chance and serendipity hardening towards destiny; moving from what could happen to what is meant to be.

I weigh his phone in my hand. I can make the connection. Everything I've seen on it lends strength to my idea, pushing me from theory towards action. I toy with it. Moment of decision. As I look at it, the light flashes, the buzzing vibration startles me. He's sent a message to himself. The message is mostly expletives, but I get the gist: he has noticed that his phone is missing and he wants it back.

That's a sign. He's made my mind up for me. I tap in a text back to him.

Ur bro has ur fone

I put the phone in my bag and get ready to go out. I have no intention of giving it back just yet. Propositions are so much better put in person. I want to know where he's living and Jamie will lead me right to him. I select *my wardrobe carefully. Striped vest, white pedal pushers, espadrilles, suitably nautical. I add a hat and dark glasses and I'm off down to the river. Sunny Saturday in July. Perfect for a boat ride.*

14

I'm not *consciously* thinking about her but ever since the first time I saw her, she's been in my head. I'm talking to Steve, he works on the boats with me, but part of my brain is ticking through possibilities. How I can meet her? Where does she live? Can I get her number? Would it look weird if I called on her? Where will I find her? Where will she be?

Steve nudges me. 'We've got a customer. Get a load of that. She's well fit!'

I look up and she is there.

He steps forward to greet her, ready with the patter. I pull him back. 'Don't even think about it. She's mine.'

I hop into the nearest punt and hold my hand out to her.

'Thank you,' she says. 'Like the hat.'

I'm wearing this stupid boater, white shirt and black trousers Alan makes us wear on Saturdays in the season. I go to take it off.

'Don't.' She looks at me, appraising, head on one side. 'It suits you, makes you look French. Italian. Something. Different, anyway.' She smiles. 'Oh, here.' She reaches into her bag. 'I've got something. Oh, no!' She searches through her bag. 'I've left it at home! It's your brother's phone. I found it on the bench where we were sitting. It must have fallen out of his pocket. I thought you might be down here. I was going to ask you to give it back to him.'

'I'm disappointed. I thought you'd come here cos of me and my punt.'

'That as well.' She holds a £20 note, folded. 'How long will this buy me?'

'As long as you like.'

I take her where we went before: down the river as far as the weir. I moor the punt and we cross on to the island. This time I'm not so shy.

I lose track of time. We are late getting back and I've lost my hat. Steve smirks and points to his watch. There's a queue. Alan is less than pleased.

'She'd better have paid you,' he says, as I get the punt ready for the next customers. 'Saturday afternoon is our busy time. I don't want you giving away no freebies. I'm not paying you to go punting pretty lasses up and down the river for free like some poncy student. Where's your hat?'

My hand goes to my head. There are willow leaves in my hair. 'Branch caught it. Went in the river. I tried to get it, but . . .' I shrug.

'That's coming out of your wages. Them hats are expensive. They don't grow on trees, you know. Belt and Braces had to order them specially.'

Belt and Braces is this old man's shop in the High Street. His brother-in-law runs it. Alan gets his clothes there. I can't look at Steve. It began with the boaters growing on trees, but the mention of Belt and Braces cracks him up.

'I don't know what you're smirking at.' Alan glares at us. 'The two of you, bad as each other, giggling like a couple of girls.'

'Sorry, Alan.' I swipe away tears. 'Private joke. I'll make the time up. Come in early. Help you open up. How would that be? And I'll pay for the boater, no problem.'

Alan's anger modifies to grumbling. 'All right. But I won't have you two larking about.' He's not very tall and he pulls himself up to his full height. 'You're here to take the customers for a ride, not me.'

He turns on his heel and goes back to his booth, well satisfied that he's had the last word. That sets Steve off again and I join in. I can't stop grinning and I'd laugh at anything. I've got a date. She's going to pick me up at eight.

I make sure I get into the bathroom before Martha. When I come out, I find her standing on the landing in her dressing gown, scowling at me. Without her make-up, she looks about ten.

'What were you *doing* in there?'

'Getting ready. All yours now.'

Her scowl deepens. 'I hope it's not all wet and messy and I hope you've cleaned out the basin. I can't stand it when it's all scummy and full of little bits of stubble. And you'd better not have been using my shampoo.'

'I've got my own, thank you. And I wiped out the basin. Just for you.'

My mood is too good for her to shake it.

'Zoe's having a party,' she says as she's passing my door. 'Lee will be there and I said I'd ask you. Do you want to come?'

'Thanks, but I've got plans.'

She stops in her tracks and walks back.

'Plans?'

'Since this afternoon. I've got a date.'

'A date?'

She's in the room now. I'm standing there, half naked. She doesn't care.

'Do you mind? I'm trying to get dressed here.'

I zip up my jeans and pull on a new T-shirt. Change my mind. Strip it off and grab a shirt from the wardrobe.

'You can't wear that!' Martha's nose wrinkles. 'You look like you're going for a job interview.'

I pull out shirts, one after another. Martha rejects them all – too smart, too casual, too school, too beach party . . .

At last she goes for a plain dark blue. Tommy Hilfiger. No wonder she likes it. She bought it for me last birthday.

118

'So?' She asks as I button it. 'Who's the date?'

I tap my nose. 'None of yours. Now, if you don't mind, I have to finish getting ready.' I scoop up some hair product and turn to the mirror to arrange my hair. 'She'll be here at eight. I don't want to be late.' I pick up my watch. 'It's nearly eight now.'

A car horn sounds outside. She's on time. I take that as a good sign. I'm out of the door and down the stairs. When I look up at my window, I see Martha staring, mouth open, catching flies. I laugh and wave. Martha does not wave back. Her mouth shuts like a trap. Her lips compress into a thin line.

'I've brought your brother's phone,' Caro says as I get in the car. She holds it out for me to see. 'It is his, I take it? I thought maybe we could drop it off on our way.'

'On our way to where?' I ask as I fasten my seat belt.

'On our way to wherever we are going.'

I give her directions and she drives off. She's driving the cream-coloured Mini convertible with the top down. It's a nice ride. If I had a car, this is the kind of car I'd like to have. I sit back and enjoy the novelty of being driven about by a girl. Some guys wouldn't like that, but I don't mind it at all. She's not a bad driver. A bit fast, but sure and decisive. Better than me, that's for certain. I've only just started taking lessons. They are expensive and Martha gets priority. Haven't even put in for my test yet.

'How come you have a car?' I ask.

'Trevor bought it for me. Seventeenth birthday present.

He taught me to drive. We used to live in a place where there was a private road. He'd take me out on that. I passed my test just after my seventeenth birthday.'

'Who's Trevor?'

'The man who is married to my mother.'

'Don't you call him Dad?'

'No, I don't.'

She speaks without taking her eyes off the road. She's wearing a short dress. Low-cut with thin straps that fall off her shoulders. Her tattoo shows black. She's driving barefoot. The slippy material rides up as she uses the pedals. I try not to look at her legs.

My brother answers second ring. He's in Adidas shorts and his Villa shirt. There's a beer in one hand, a joint in the other, a pizza box open on the coffee table, football on the widescreen telly.

'Not going out then?'

'Nah.' He takes a swig from his can. 'Can't be arsed. Having a quiet night. Want to join me? I got pizza. Diablo with extra cheese. Villa versus Juventus has just started and I've got plenty of beers.'

'Nah, I'm good.' I shake my head. 'Another time. I've got a date tonight. Just brought your phone round.'

'Ha. One mystery solved.' He grins. 'I sent a text from Carl's phone to the arsehole who took it, and got this message saying you had it. Weird or what? I couldn't text you cos I didn't have your number.'

'Here.' I give it back to him.

He looks at it like it's the Rossetta Stone.

'Thanks, man. My entire life is in here.'

'You should take better care of it.'

'When you're shit-faced, you kind of lose track.' He continues to stare at it, flicking through the apps. 'Who'd got it?'

'The girl who found you last night.'

'What girl?' He really must have been out of it.

'She's sitting in the car outside.'

'Oh, *that* girl.' He looks past me. He does remember. 'I was wondering who would go out with you. Second mystery solved. Where you off to?'

'She's taking me for a ride.'

He grins with the good side of his mouth. 'You be careful, then. Got enough of these?' He scoops packets of condoms from a dish Gran used to keep sweets in for us.

'For God's sake, Rob!' Despite myself, I blush. 'I've got some.'

'You can never have too many.' He stuffs a wad of them into my shirt pocket. 'Here. You might get lucky. Don't do anything I wouldn't do. That doesn't leave you with much.'

His phone goes.

'Aren't you going to answer it?'

He checks the number. 'Yes, sure.'

I glance back through the window as I go down the path to where Caro is waiting for me. The big TV is a patch of vivid green. The screen changes to a blur of team colours.

The crowd rises. I can hear the roar through the glass. Someone's scored but Rob's not looking. He's still talking on his phone, staring after me. Sometimes he looks just like Martha.

'Everything OK?' she asks.

She slips her phone into her bag as I get into the car.

'Sure. Everything is good.'

I lean forward to get into the low seat and the condoms spill out of my shirt pocket, falling into the foot well in a multicoloured cascade of little foil-covered packages.

'Came prepared, I see,' she says, with one eyebrow raised. At least I've made her smile. She hasn't smiled all that often.

'It was Rob. He, er –' I sound like a kid blaming his big brother. I scrabble to retrieve them, more to hide my blushes than anything else.

'Where are you taking me?' I ask as I stuff the packets I can find into my jeans' pocket and try to rewind to the moment I got into the car.

'It's a secret,' she says.

I turn back and see Rob's still at the window watching as she drives off.

15

I've driven past Beldon Hill plenty of times, but never climbed up it, especially not at night carrying a hamper and a blanket. It's set off the main road. She turns on to a farm track and follows that until it more or less runs out. We have to walk then. She climbs a stile. I follow her into a field. The hill rears above us. At the top, the grass glows golden in the last of the sun. A few solitary trees crouch at the summit, bent by the wind. Their shadows are lengthening. The wooded flanks are already in semi-darkness.

'Are we going all the way to the top?'

'It'll be worth it, you'll see,' she replies over her shoulder. 'There's a full moon tonight. We won't need a torch.'

She points and there's the moon, hanging huge in the sky like a pale balloon, the seas and mountains showing clearly, puckering the surface. I hadn't noticed it before. I stand for a moment, gazing at it.

It's a struggle to get to the top, but she is right. It is worth it. A few sheep regard us with strange, slotted eyes, then turn back to cropping at the drying grass. She spreads the blanket for us. The sun has nearly gone now. Just a red gleam in the west, contained within a lens of pinkish clouds. The sky above us is darkening to purple, the first of the stars newly visible. The motorway shows way in the distance, a snaking necklace of lights, its roar reduced to a low-grade hum.

She takes off her sandals and walks about, arms wide, as if she's about to fly.

'I love it up here,' she says. 'I love high places.' She comes back to me and sits opposite, arms clasped round her bare legs. 'This place is special, do you know that? I come here as often as I can. Different times of day. Sometimes in the very early morning. I come to watch the sun rising, or in the evening to see it set. I've been taking photographs, trying to capture the moment of transition night to day, day to night. I like margins. It's different depending on the time of day, time of year. It can be weird, spooky here, especially in fog or mist, or when the clouds come down. You see things . . .'

Her voice tails off. I look around. It seems perfectly normal to me.

'Some people won't come up here in the daytime, let alone at night. There was a notorious murder. Years ago. A woman was found hanging inside a hollow tree. Some say it was witchcraft. Witches gather here . . .'

'What? Nowadays?' I laugh, wondering if she is having me on. 'You're kidding me!'

'No, I'm not. Look at that.' She points to a circle where the grass has been blackened by fire. 'That's left from Midsummer.'

'You'll be telling me that there are fairies here next.'

'Of course there are! See that lone thorn?' She nods towards the top of the hill. 'That's a fairy tree. It's very old because no one dare cut it down.'

'Even now?'

'Even now. They live under the hill. Can't you feel their presence?'

She comes crawling towards me across the blanket. I can't tell if she's serious or teasing and I don't care. She's very near and I can't decide whether her eyes are brown or green, or a mixture of the two, then she's kissing me.

I go to hold her but she's up and out of my grip. She strips off her dress. She's not wearing knickers or a bra. I wish I'd known that before. She walks away, to the edge of the hill, then she comes back towards me, stepping lightly on the springing grass, her body silver in the moon-light, the tattoo on her shoulder like a tarnished star.

'Come on. Take yours off, too.'

I hadn't been expecting that.

'What, me? Someone might see!'

'Don't be daft!'

Her laugh is like silver bells chiming. I look up at her. The night is coming on fast now. She glimmers in the half-light. This place is so quiet, even the sheep have stopped cropping. There's a mist creeping over the grass, low to the ground and curling round her ankles, like she's bringing it with her. I move back slightly, flinching away, as though I'm afraid of her, and maybe I am a little bit. She's a strange one. I've never met anyone like her. All that talk about fairies. A little part of me is left wondering if she is quite real.

'You're not *afraid*, are you?'

She interprets my movement, but keeps on coming towards me with the same slow, light, undulating step. She smiles. Even that is disconcerting. Slightly too wide; the eyes too knowing. It is the smile you would give to a child.

''Course not.' I find myself regressing, growing petulant.

I move back a bit more. I *am* afraid, but for a whole other reason. One I can hardly admit to myself, let alone to her.

'What is the matter, then?' She's almost on me now.

'Nothing.'

I pull her down on top of me and I don't feel like a child any more.

We kiss for a while. Her mouth is soft and warm. I move to shift our positions, but she stops me.

'Let's get rid of this lot.' She pulls at my shirt and my belt buckle. As I take my jeans off, all the condoms fall out of my pocket again.

'Good thing you came prepared . . .'

She laughs and I join in. Joke shared. The laughter

126

dispels my awkwardness and I'm soon as naked as she is.
I forget that people might be watching. What people?
Where? I forget about the sheep, I forget about everything
except the feel of her skin against mine, the smell of her
hair, the prickle of the grass against my back, the hard-
ness of the ground beneath my knees. Then every other
sensation is erased and I'm concentrating on one thing
and one thing only.

When it's over, I lie back and stare up at the blackness
above me. The stars are fully out now. They seem nearer
up here, thickly scattered. I look for the ones I know.

'What are you looking at?'

I show her Venus, bright in the west. Deneb, Vega,
Altair, Arcturus, the Twins – Castor and Pollux.

'Do you know the zodiac signs?'

'Of course. There's Leo.' I point to the west. 'Virgo,
Libra and Scorpio going down to the south.'

'Leo. That's me.'

'Do you believe in all that?'

'Used to take an interest. What's your sign?'

'I'm Sagittarius. Down there near the southern horizon.
You can't see me too well from here.'

She is sitting up, arms wrapped round her knees looking down at me. I can't believe this is happening. I can't
look at her. I have to look back at the stars.

I'd never been naked with a girl. Isn't that weird? My
past encounters had been in bedrooms at parties, in the

woods, in the park, behind the garages, anywhere private and dark. Only the most necessary garments removed or loosened. I had more than a rough idea. I've seen plenty of porn mags, DVDs and Internet sites, some of it pretty hard core. But she is different. She has grace and beauty. Her body is delicate and slender; her breasts small but perfectly shaped, her belly concave under ribs defined by shadows. She is the finest thing that I have ever seen. It makes all the rest false and tawdry, like one of those blow-up dolls. I hadn't been with many girls. Technically, I was a virgin. Suzy would always panic at the last minute and push me away. That's what I was afraid to tell her. Afraid she'd know. That she would guess. She's been with lots of guys. How do I measure up?

'You don't have to worry,' she says, as if she knows what I'm thinking.

We put our clothes back on and she opens the hamper. It contains a bottle of champagne and two glasses. 'It's my birthday,' she says, pouring until the bubbles run over. 'Cheers.'

'Your birthday!' I raise my glass to her. 'You didn't say anything.'

'It wasn't my birthday then. It is now.'

We drink the champagne.

'Empty.' She holds up the bottle. 'Time to go.'

We walk back across the fields. There's light from the moon and stars, but it's still pretty black. She leads me, like she can see in the dark.

'You don't have to go home, do you?' she asks when we get to the car.

I shake my head. I have my cover story if needed. Stayed over at Cal's.

'What about you?'

'My mother won't notice. She never gets up 'til it's time to go out. Sunday is brunch day.' She starts the car, the sound of the engine sudden and loud. 'Let's go somewhere.'

When she gets to the motorway, the road opens in front of us, wide with possibilities. I want her to drive for ever, never go back.

Of course, that doesn't happen.

She drives for a while, then says, 'I'm hungry.'

She pulls off the motorway and stops at a greasy spoon caravan parked in a lay-by. *The Snack Shack Phil's Grill's – Open All Hours.* The sign is hand-painted on the side of the van; the menu in Dulux gloss on a broken piece of hardboard: *Breakfast Roll's Everything On,* the letters drippy like their eggs.

The man smiles and gives her an extra slice of bacon. There's a bit of chat going forward and back. He knows her. He winks at me over the top of her head. He says something, but I don't hear him. Instead I hear Rob's voice sneering.

You didn't think you were the only one?

I juggle the roll, piled up with bacon, sausage, egg and a ladle of beans. The bean juice trickles warm on my

129

wrist and I spill sauce down my shirt. The sign was right about 'everything on'. I'm hungry, too, starving, but the food wads in my mouth. I choke and can't swallow. I have to spit it out into the bin. I take a swig of scalding coffee. It's watery and tastes of nothing. The top is filmed with grease, specked with grit from the lay-by. Traffic flashes by. I breathe a mix of dust and diesel and wish I'd had tea instead.

'Do you come here often?' I ask her, making it sound light like a joke but I really want to know. I want to know if she has come here with other guys after a night out under the stars or in some other place, like a motel, say. There's a sign for one, pointing down the road. I don't ask her anything like that, of course. I just smile a bit weakly and pretend to tear another chunk out of my roll all the time wondering when I can chuck it.

'Now and again,' she says.

'Who with?' I ask.

I didn't mean to ask that. It just came out.

She throws away her roll which gives me the excuse to bin mine, too. She wipes her mouth, then her hands. The napkins are shiny and thin, not likely to mop up much of anything.

'What do you care? I'm with you now.'

She kisses me, her lips sweet with ketchup.

We drive back into town. They are doing work on the bridge, replacing a section of the parapet. Part of the road is coned off. The temporary traffic lights stay on red for an age. I want them to stay that way, just so I can sit in the car with her.

She drops me at the end of the road with a 'See you'.

'When?' I ask but she doesn't seem to hear. She just checks the mirror and she's gone.

16

Sorry to do it to you Jimbo but you did lead her right to me. She's been round to see me since and I have to admit to giving her one for old times' sake. Got to hand it to you – I thought you were on to a loser with that one when I saw who you were eyeing in the bar – so it was a bit of a surprise when I saw her sitting in the car outside the house. She called me while you were busy stuffing the rubbers in your pocket. I hadn't seen her for a while but I knew she'd be back.

She's different. This isn't the Caro I remember. Some things don't change. She's still mad as a box of frogs but she's gone all political. She's telling me all this stuff and sounding like Martha – but a lot more extreme – if you know what I mean. That's the thing about her – she don't do things by halves. I try to shut her up but she's not having any.

ME: I'm not interested in all that shit.

HER: You ought to be. Look what they've done to you!

Then she's off again so I zone out and I'm thinking what a lucky little dog you are to pop your cherry with her. None better. This goes on for a while then she stops.

HER: Have you even been listening?

ME: No I ain't.

Looks like she might start again – so I distract her only way I know how.

Afterwards she's looking at my scars tracing them with her finger and asking how I got them – wanting me to tell her what happened exactly.

ME: Don't really remember.

This is what I generally say.

HER: Course you do.

ME: Yeah – well – I don't like talking about it.

HER: You've got to get things out sometimes.

I look to see if she's taking the piss – you never know with her – but she's acting like she's genuinely interested and really wants to know – like she cares about me and I want her to care. Sometimes I surprise even myself.

ME: I'm keeping a video diary, y'know? Like I used to.

HER: That's a good idea – people ought to know what's going on, what's really happening, from the people on the ground out there. People like you.

ME: My memory ain't altogether reliable. Time runs

differently for different people – fast for some – others see it all in slo-mo.

HER: Yeah. I understand that. How does it run for you?

I start to tell her and I'm back there.

We are out on routine patrol approaching some little shit town. The WMIK drops us and we fan out each side of the road – me and Mac on the right. The house on our side looks deserted – two small windows either side of a door like a kid's drawing. The entrance is covered by one of those plastic curtains – red and yellow strips slightly moving – clashing softly together – like there's a through breeze or maybe someone moving in there creating a draught displacing the air or a muzzle stirring the strips. Something's not right about it. I motion for Mac, who's in front of me, to go down to the side of the building out of the direct line of fire and edge along the walls. He takes one more step and I hear a series of little tiny tones like someone dialling on a mobile then a metallic click. I know what it is – the pressure plate of an IED making contact – but too late to do anything about it. I'm thrown back right up into the air. Mac's in front of me. He takes the full force. I can't hear anything – my head's ringing with the blast and the dust is so thick all around us that the sun is just a smudge of light. I can smell cordite and burnt fabric and something else – like Sunday roast. It catches in my throat – makes me cough and gag as I grope towards where I think he might be – feeling with my hands cos I can't see. I can tell he's hurt bad. He's lost his leg – blown right off halfway up the thigh. I get a tourniquet on to him, all the time with rounds coming in. I still can't hear a thing but I can see little puffs in the dust and chips flying off the wall. My right leg is pretty mashed – numb and useless – but I can crawl. He can do nothing at all – I grab him by the webbing and begin pulling him back. The WMIK's coming under heavy fire itself, the lads pinned down fully engaged laying down rounds. All I'm thinking is to get Mac back or near enough for them to come and get us – which they did.

We got him out of there and he lived. He lost one leg completely – the other off at the knee. Seemed all right last time I saw him – looking to the future. He's coping better than me – ironic really. They gave me a medal for what I done – so I'm a genuine hero – but like someone said – medals cast deep shadows. I kept both my legs but I lost something else out there. When the thing went off right in front of us – the noise deafened me – I couldn't hear. Couldn't see. A kind of darkness came over me and everything seemed very far away – like I was in a tunnel so full of dust it's like the light had gone out and I couldn't breathe. When I dream about it that's what wakes me. I snapped out of it then cos I had to help Mac but now it's like the darkness is back – creeping over me a bit more every day. I don't see a future – there *is* no future. I have no purpose – no reason to be. All I'm doing is marking time. I got no right to feel like this. I'm still here ain't I – with two arms, two legs, tackle intact. I think about

Johnny Boy – not coming back – and Mac and I feel shame for being the way I am. I don't feel entitled to help of any kind. If I believed in that sort of thing – I'd say I was damned. As it is I might be all right on the outside but inside I'm broke beyond anybody's fixing. There's no help for me.

I don't mean to tell her the last bit. It just comes out – she don't act shocked or surprised. She don't say anything. She gets out of bed and goes – not even a 'See you'. Then after she's gone I lie there and it's like she's opened a valve in my head that I can't shut off. It's like the nightmares I have but worse cos I'm awake. My ears are ringing like after the explosion and I ache – not just my leg but my back and my arms and my head. I wasn't even wounded there but my head hurts worst of all.

17

*'Protest is when I say this does not please me.
Resistance is when I ensure what does not
please me occurs no more.'*
Ulrike Meinhof (attrib.)

*We tried protest. Now it is time for resistance. Time for
action. The plan is coming together in my mind. At
first, it seemed like a mad dream but now it seems
eminently possible. I can see a way to achieve it.
Everything is falling into place, like it has been pre-
ordained. They've gone to France. No idea when they
are coming back. So I have the house to myself and can
do exactly as I like. I can sleep all day, if I want to. Stay
out all night. Go away without telling anybody where
I'm going, without having to explain. I hate explaining.
I can eat what I like, or not eat anything if I don't want.
Drink as much as I like and what I like. I've already
started on the Moet.*

*I've got plenty of cash. She's left me £300 guilt money
and Trevor's given me my very own credit card. He gave
it to me on the quiet, imagining a public announcement*

wouldn't go down too well. He imagined right there. She'd go apeshit. But she's not going to know.

'Our little secret.'

I will put this card to very good use.

'I know I'm not your real dad,' he says, but I think he wishes he was. He likes to spoil me. When we are out together, he looks proud, like he wants people to think that I belong to him. And he buys me things; he likes to spend 'just us' time without her. I make sure the things he buys are expensive, very expensive, and that the things we do together are things that I want to do.

He's taught me to drive and he's bought me a car, so I have independence. He's also into shooting and he's taught me. Useful things to know.

Back to the matter in hand:

PRAXIS

An interesting word.

Praxis: the process by which a theory, lesson, or skill is enacted or practised, embodied and/or realised.

I interpret this to mean that I need an expert, someone who has the skill to put theory into practice. I've got just the guy.

18

At first I'm happy, really, really happy. Then I'm not. I go home in a daze, get through that day, just waiting for the night to come. But she doesn't show that night, or the next, or the next. I go from euphoria to deep depression. I check my phone every five minutes. No messages and I don't know her number. I look her up on Facebook. She's not even on it. Everyone I *know* is on it. Everyone in the whole world is on it. I check all the other sites. Nothing. She doesn't exist in cyberspace.

I mope about, Martha calls it sulking, but Mum doesn't even notice. She's stopped worrying about Rob for the time being. He went with her to see Grandpa and even thanked her for her latest food parcel. She came back beaming.

'He seems different. More settled. He's got Grandpa's car back on the road and he's been working the allotment.

He seems much more focused, as though he's gained a sense of purpose.'

'Like what?' Martha asks.

'He didn't say.'

'Getting himself a job, by any chance? He's perfectly capable.'

'I dare say he will when the right opportunity comes along. He certainly seems to be steadying down. You know, I wouldn't be surprised if he'd got a girlfriend.'

'Girlfriend! Rob!' Martha snorts her astonishment. 'What makes you think that!'

'Oh, I don't know. Something. Call it mother's intuition.'

'Well, I'd get it checked if I was you. What girl would be mad enough to go out with him?'

'You'd be surprised. He's smartened himself up quite a bit. He can look very handsome and he can be charming when he makes the effort.' Rob is Mum's favourite, no doubt. 'It's about time he settled down. Started thinking about a family, even. Lots of boys his age do. Are you going out tonight?' she asks. I shake my head. 'It's just me and Jack are going out to the Miller's for a drink and a bite to eat. We won't be late. You can come if you like.'

I shake my head again. I don't go out at night, in case *she* turns up for me, or in case I see her out with somebody else. I fantasise about seeing her with the Art guy. I think about ripping his face off.

This goes on for a week. Two. I think she may turn up

at the boats. I'm there early and leave late. Alan thinks it's devotion to duty. It's hardly that. I scrutinise the crowds who come down to the river, hoping to see her, my heart thumps hard in my chest every time I spot a girl who looks anything like her. When I get a fare, I sweep up and back, poling like a maniac, just in case she's waiting for me back at the station.

'Steady!' Alan says as I bring the punt in too fast, jolting the elderly couple who stagger out, their clothes blotched with splashes. The man complains. Alan offers their money back. 'What's the matter with you? he says. 'It'll come out of your wages . . .'

He goes on, but I'm not listening. I'm scanning the crowds again. It's August now. More tourists. More people down by the river. I make excuses about a wrist injury. He puts me on the station, taking the money. That suits me fine. From here, I can watch all the time.

Just when I've given up. There she is. I'm lying on my bed in my boxers, listening to music. I wouldn't want anyone else hearing the mix – love songs on shuffle. I even raided Martha's iTunes when she was out. I've got my earpieces in and I'm so deep in the songs that I don't hear anything from the outside, even Martha hammering on the door. She comes in and touches my shoulder, making me jump a mile. She yanks my earpieces out.

'Your girlfriend's outside. Can't you hear? She'll have the whole street out!'

She's standing arms folded, glaring down at me. She looks like Mum. Sounds like Mum, too.

I can hear the horn and I'm off the bed and at the window. There she is. She looks up at me and grins, beckoning me down to her. I grab some clothes, hopping round the room trying to ram my legs into jeans, pulling on a shirt, jamming my feet into trainers and I'm off down the stairs, through the door and down the path.

When I look up at my window, Martha is there, frowning down at us, arms tightly folded. I give her a wave. I'm happy. I want to share it. She's not even looking at me.

Caro returns the stare, lowering her sunglasses, sketching a wave with a flip of her fingers. Martha's frown deepens. I look from one to the other. It's a hot night but I can feel the chill like a frost field between them.

'What *is* it with you and Martha?'

'What do you mean?' She looks away then to start the car. 'What makes you think there is anything between me and Martha?'

'Just a feeling. Didn't you used to be friends, or something?'

'Or something.' She repeats my words, says nothing more.

'Yeah. You were.' I go on, prompting her. 'You must have been to be invited to her birthday. She doesn't invite just anybody.'

'Maybe I was. I don't remember a thing about it,' she says it like it's too boring to even think about and stares straight ahead, cutting the conversation dead. It's as if she has turned herself off.

I try a different tack, hoping to get her talking about something else.

'How's your day been?' I ask, following up with a similar set of questions.

'What have you been up to?'

'Been anywhere?'

'Done anything interesting?'

Things like that. The last one sounds pretty lame, the sort of thing your gran would ask you. Her answers are non-committal or non-existent. I shut up then and we lapse into silence. In my head I'm hearing a parallel set of questions.

Where have you been since I last saw you?

Why didn't you call me?

Why didn't you message me?

Are you seeing someone?

What did you do with them? The same as you did with me?

These questions are there in my mind all the time, like mosquitoes, whining and insistent, but I don't ask them. There's someone else. I know. I can feel it. But I don't ask her. I don't say anything because she wouldn't tell me. I'm learning about her. Not much, but some. She operates on a strictly need to know basis. She lies and doesn't care if you know it. She doesn't gossip and chatter. She doesn't say much at all as a general rule, so what she does say counts. So does what she doesn't say, which might even be more important.

I sit back in the seat. Traffic is crawling through town. The temporary lights on the bridge slowing everything down. I wonder where we are going. She probably wouldn't tell me, even if she knew. She's not in the mood for talking, so while we are waiting, I let my mind drift back to the time she seems to be denying. The time when she and Martha were friends and she came to Martha's birthday.

It must have been Martha's fifteenth. There was a big rumpus because Mum said she was too young to go out with her mates, so she had to make do with a film and a pizza. I wasn't invited, not that I was bothered. Rob was home on leave and we watched the Villa in his room. They were coming back for a sleepover – cue for us to keep well out of the way.

In the morning, I came down to find Mum talking to one of the collecting mothers.

'Just went. Middle of the night. I was worried. You hear such awful stories.'

'Is she all right?'

'Apparently. I called her mother. She had to go home.' She dropped her voice to a murmur. All I caught was *a bit of an accident* and e*mbarrassed*. They got in a huddle, talking low: *girls, that time, awkward*.

The other mother nodded as if she knew. I didn't, so I sidled closer. Mum saw me and that stopped the conversation altogether. I got told to stop hovering and get my own

146

breakfast. Mum spoke sharply, frowning at me as if I'd done something wrong. I was still wondering what kind of accident, when the penny dropped. This was some secret female thing that boys were not supposed to know about; that's why they were whispering and glowering at me.

I coloured up at the thought of it and got busy with the cereal packets. I didn't know much about periods but what I did know made me glad that I was a boy.

So she came to a sleepover and didn't stay. Is that the source of the enmity between her and Martha? Could be. Martha can be very touchy. There has to be more to it. There always is. If there was a row, they were quiet about it. The girls round the table were as listless as revenants in the sunshine, not up to noticing anything much, but Caro's departure was news to them. One of them asked 'Isn't she here?' as if she might have crept under a piece of furniture or spent the night in the cupboard under the stairs. Girls are always falling out over something, the patterns of their friendships change, alliances shift. Friends are lost, new ones made, but usually not for ever, the kaleidoscope twists and before you know it, they're back together. After that night she disappeared from Martha's life altogether.

Something happened that night. Something Caro doesn't want to talk about.

I expect her to drive out into the country. We are heading in that direction. Once she crosses the bridge, she takes one of the ribbon roads out of town. We've gone about a mile or so, when she suddenly turns the wheel and takes a left into an estate.

'I feel like a night in.'

She turns right, then left, then right again, screeching round corners, bouncing over traffic-calming devices following the maze of closes, slaloming through another Legoland development. It is quite a lot like ours, except the houses are bigger, posher – all detached with drive-ways and double, even triple, garages. The cars parked in the drives are Mercs, BMWs, a few Porsches, lots of SUVs.

The roads are named after the trees that have been ripped up to make way for all these executive houses: Oak Close, Ash Road, Beech Avenue, The Limes. She lives on Cypress Drive. She stops and the electric gates swing open. She sweeps round a little, circular drive towards the porticoed front door. Her house is called 'The Stables' and is set slightly apart, bigger than the rest. It's like a cut-down stately home.

'Nice,' I say.

'No, it's not. It's naff.' She parks anywhere and swings her legs out of the car. 'It's somewhere to live. That's all.'

I walk in behind her. Everything is in various shades of beige and oatmeal. Very tasteful. I fight an impulse to take my shoes off. She takes me into the living room: cream carpet, huge leather sofas, smoked-glass coffee table. The room is wide and long with an L-shaped dining area, where there's another smoked-glass table with high-backed chairs drawn up to it and a bowl of fruit set in the centre. A door leads to a conservatory.

'It looks like a show house,' I say.

'It is. That's why mother bought it.' She gestures around. 'Furniture. Pictures. Everything.'

I stand in the middle of the room not sure what I should do. It's like we've both arrived at a party and no one else has turned up.

'Do you want a drink?' She presses a button in the sideboard. A panel slides back to show a bank of bottles. 'There's everything, really. Oh, except tequila. I seem to have drunk most of that.'

'Got any vodka?' I don't really like tequila. Too oily.

'It's in the freezer. I'll go and get it.'

I walk over to a big cabinet which takes up one wall of the room. Inside it are lots of trophies. She comes back with a bottle of Absolut, the frost forming on it, and two glasses, misted and smoking with ice.

'What are these?' I tap the glass encasing the trophies. 'They didn't come with the house.'

'They're Trevor's,' she says as she pours two hefty shots of vodka.

'Oh.' I don't ask her about her real dad. I don't suppose she'd tell me, even if I did. Instead, I go on with the trophy conversation. 'What did he get them for?'

'Shooting.'

'Shooting?'

'Yes.'

'With guns?'

'No, pea-shooters. What do you think?'

'Does he have any here? Guns, I mean.'

'Of course.'

'What kinds?'

'All kinds: hunting rifles, a shotgun, a couple of hand-guns – a Glock 9mm and a Colt M1911.'

'It's illegal to own handguns,' I say. I know that because Grandpa had to turn his in.

She shrugs. 'That's why they're kept locked up.'

'What is he? Some kind of gangster?'

'No, he's an estate agent. He just likes guns, that's all. He collects them.'

'Can you shoot?'

'Yes. I'm not a bad standard.' She might have been talking about Grade 8 on the clarinet. 'My mother doesn't like it. That's why I do it.'

'Doesn't she like guns?'

'No, not so much.'

When she comes back, I pull out the cigarette case Cal found in a junk shop and take out a couple of joints. These are some I rolled earlier. I've been raiding Rob's stash. She has no objection, rather the opposite, but we go into the conservatory. She doesn't like the smell of smoke in the house.

I prefer it in there. The floor is shiny cream tiles and I'm not so afraid of spilling anything. It's full of rattan furniture and plants. Some of them are big – tree size.

There's a water feature running down into a pond. I catch a flash of colour. It has fish in it.

She sets the bottle down on top of a copy of *House & Garden*.

'Where are they, your mum and stepdad?' I ask.

'Gone away,' she says, eyes narrowed as she lights a rollie, touching the lighter flame to the twisted end. She inhales, then blows out a thin stream of smoke. 'We've got a place in France. They've gone there.'

'Leaving you on your own?'

'I'm eighteen, not eight. Anyway, they think I'm going away to Cornwall with friends.'

'Like Martha and her mates?'

'Yeah. As if. Can you see me in a caravan in Newquay? Shows how much my mother knows about me.'

She takes another toke on the spliff.

It might be the weed, it might be her mother, it might be the thought of Martha and her mates that's making her frown and bite her lip.

'We could go away if you want,' I say. 'I've got a tent. Well, I know where I can get one.'

Wrong thing to say.

'I don't actually *want* to go anywhere,' she says, speaking slowly and very clearly, as if I'm a bit dim or hard of hearing, or possibly both. 'I made up the story for the benefit of my mother. She doesn't have to feel guilty then and will leave me alone. Suits her anyway, she doesn't want "the children" there. It would cramp her style.'

151

'What about your brother?' I ask, trying to change the direction of the conversation. I don't want to piss her off. It's not a good thing to do if you're hoping to have sex with someone. I know that much.

'*Step*brother,' she corrects. 'She's packed the poor little sod off to some kind of fat camp.' She throws the spliff away and comes over to sit astride me. 'So I'm on my own.'

The rattan proves kind of fragile. There's a crack that sounds like the cane is splitting. We both fall about laughing and move to the living room, leaving our clothes behind us. Next we move to the kitchen.

She wants to have sex in every room in the house and it is a big house. We end up in her room, where I pretty much pass out.

When I wake up, she's not in the bed with me. I've no idea what time it is. It feels very late or pretty early. It's hard to tell. I turn the light on and look around. She must have gone through a Goth phase. Her room is very dark. The walls are painted purple and the blinds are black.

One wall is all pictures. There are faces looking down, faces I don't recognise. They are good-looking enough to be film stars, but I don't think they are. They look young, but the photographs are all in black and white, like they were taken a long time ago. The scenes could be contemporary: demonstrations, police on the streets; a bomb-damaged car, just wheels and twisted metal, and people climbing over rubble, bodies and carnage, like from a war zone, but these are images from another time, not now. In the middle is a symbol that I don't recognise with the letters RAF on it but I don't think it's anything to do with the Royal Air Force. Their emblem isn't a red star and a Kalashnikov.

There's a Palestinian flag hanging down and recent pictures taken off the Internet of people marching through the streets of Cairo, fighting in Libya and Syria, demonstrating in Gaza and on the West Bank. Propped in a corner of the room are a bunch of placards with a police riot helmet hanging like a trophy from one of them. Above that are colour photos torn from newspapers: people marching through London, smashed windows, fires in the street. In the centre is a blown-up press picture of Caro wearing the helmet, visor up, yelling, giving the finger.

She's got lots of books. Shelves of them. There are a couple on art, some poetry, novels, and quite a few on politics and philosophy – Nietzsche, Karl Marx . . . Heavy stuff. Others I've never even heard of, like Bakunin, Carlos Marighella. I'll have to check them out on the Internet. If she wants to do Politics at uni, she's certainly getting a head start and if I'm going to stand a chance of understanding her, I'll have to do some homework.

I scout the room for more clues. There are no personal photographs of her with her family or with friends on a night out, none of the girly knick-knacks that Martha has in her room. She must keep her make-up and stuff in the bathroom. There's nothing on the dressing table except a bottle of Chanel perfume. On her desk is a laptop. I'm tempted. That could be more revealing. I listen out. The shower is running. I open it and power up. I don't get past the screensaver. Red star and Kalashnikov.

'Naughty, naughty! That's private.' I didn't hear her come in and start, guilty at getting caught. 'Not that you'd get any further. Everything is password-protected.'

'What's the screensaver?'

'RAF. Stands for Red Army Faction.'

'Who are they?'

'*Were.* Known erroneously as the Baader-Meinhof Gang.' She says it like she's giving a lecture. 'They were active in Germany in the Seventies.'

I look blank. 'What did they do?'

'They were urban guerrillas. They robbed banks, kidnapped, killed people, bombed buildings. Anything to disrupt the system. That's them up there on the wall.'

I look up at the young faces in the old black-and-white photos.

'Who's that? The one on the left?' She's pretty, her dark hair cut just below chin length. 'She looks a lot like you.'

'That's Petra Schelm.' She comes over and shuts down the laptop. 'Seriously, Jamie. It's not OK to pry.'

'OK. OK.' I swing round on the chair. 'Just curious.' I point at the photo of her in the policeman's helmet. 'You are very photogenic.'

She nods, as if that is a given. 'It was in all the papers at the time.'

'I'm bored. Distract me.' I make a grab for her but she pulls her bathrobe round her and she shakes her head.

'No. Time for you to go.'

'But you said your folks were away.'

'They are.'

'Then why?'

I get up and go over to her. I can't believe she's about to throw me out. It was not just about having sex. I want to sleep with her. Spend the whole night together. In a bed.

'I don't like sleeping with people,' she says. 'I have to sleep on my own. It's not to do with you.'

I go over to the window and part the blinds. The sky is paling at the margins, somewhere near a bird has started to sing.

'It's nearly light.'

'Time you were off, then.'

I play for time, picking up some stones I find scattered along her windowsill.

'Leave those alone.'

I turn them over, examining the markings. 'What are they?'

'Rune stones.'

'No shit!' I shake them in my cupped hands. 'What do you use them for?'

'I don't use them for anything. They're just painted pebbles. Put them back where you found them.'

I let them fall.

I don't know what makes me hang around. I go to the end of the road and turn back. The gates are shut. No chance of re-entry, the alarm light is blinking, and I'm facing a long walk across town, but I can't go yet. I look through the bars. No lights in the house. No movement. I look around, suddenly nervous at the idea of CCTV cameras – this is just the kind of estate that would have them looking out for suspicious characters loitering about just like I am now. My first instinct is to throw my hood up, but that would look even more suspicious, they would be down from the station in a minute. I can't make myself walk away. I sit on a nearby wall, light a spliff and wonder about what I'm doing and why I'm doing it. Being near her is not enough, but it is something, I guess.

I'm off, eyes closed, and drifting, thinking about her, then I hear a car starting. The mechanical click and whine of gates. My eyes snap open. I don't want to be caught watching, by anybody, least of all by her. I hop off the wall and back into the shadows behind a tree, hoping it will be enough to hide me. I don't want her thinking that I'm a nutter. A stalker.

She stops and looks left and right, even though there is no traffic. Where is she going? She pulls away without even looking in my direction. I'm on foot. I can hardly run after her. I have to let her go. I start walking. I hear the car accelerate then slow, then accelerate again. It's so quiet that I hear the engine sound for a long time. Engines sound different. Grandpa taught me that. With practice, you can tell one from another. Dogs do it easily. I stand still in the middle of the street, turning, trying to track her, trying to unplait her from the other sounds around. Seems like she's heading into town, but I can't swear to that. Eventually, the sound fades and becomes indistinguishable, blending into the distant noise of the traffic on the bypass.

19

How can two brothers be so different? Jamie is inquisitive, sensitive. Intuitive. Wants to know everything, but ignores what is right in front of him. Rob's the opposite. He doesn't ask anything but I end up telling him. He's the same way with me. Tit for tat.

He goes straight over to the shooting trophies, like Jamie did, they are hard to miss, but he doesn't ask questions or comment. Just asks:

'Where are they?'

I take him upstairs and unlock the gun cabinet. He takes the guns off the rack one at a time and inspects each one carefully. When he does this, he's like a different person – no messing, no joking, no wisecracks. He doesn't say anything but handles each gun in a quick, sure way. His movements are deft and instinctive; the weapons look like part of him.

'These are legal. He has permits!' I nod. 'Where does he keep the others?' he asks.

We are in Trevor's study. Trevor is so deeply ordinary. Wouldn't say 'boo' normally. The handguns are his one transgression. He's a collector. Owning them is illegal but he can't resist the lure of possession. Having them gives him a thrill. She thinks that they are non-firing replicas. I know they are not. He keeps them in a safe along with the bullets, heavy in the hand, snug and lethal. The safe is behind one of the pictures on the wall. I know the combination.

Rob takes out each gun, examines it, working the mechanism, feeling the heft of it, seeing how it feels in his grip.

'Sound pieces. Bullets?'

'In there with them.'

He takes out a box and shakes it, nodding to himself, then he puts it all back. I shut the heavy steel door and spin the wheels on the lock.

Rob is the perfect instrument but like the safe, I have to get the right sequence for the tumblers to fall into place. He's not very receptive to political argument. I have tried that and he either falls about laughing or pretends to go to sleep. When I point out what's happening right now, out on the streets he says, 'Send the lads in.' He's conflicted. When I talk to him about soldiers and the illegal wars in Iraq and Afghanistan, I can see that he's listening but he won't admit any interest. He understands perfectly. In his own way he's as clever as *his siblings. It's just that with anything serious, his instinct is always to take the piss.*

I have to find another combination. I work on my own ways to release his rage, to channel all that violence into constructive action.

You show me yours. I'll show you mine.

My dad went out one day and never came back. He went off as normal to go to work, except he never made it. He hadn't made it to the office for a while. In fact, there was no office. Hadn't been for months. He'd been sacked, pending investigations for fraud. That all came out afterwards. Where did he go when he was supposed to be at work? What did he do all day? Maybe he just drove around, up and down the motorways, sat in cafes, parked up in lay-bys waiting for the day to go. Who knows?

He went out that day like any other day. I'd like to say that he kissed us goodbye, but it didn't happen like that. They weren't speaking. Hadn't been for a while. He slept apart. I remember the spare room showed definite signs of habitation. His shoes were under the bed in there. His pyjamas on the pillow. His brush was on the bureau, along with bits of change, crumpled handkerchiefs, pocket detritus lying where he dropped it. I hardly saw him. He'd become like a shadow in his own house.

'He's busy with work.' That's what she said.

We used to go out, spend time together as a family.

Take picnics to Beldon Hill. My mother would sunbathe while I did roly-polies down the hill. He'd chase after me, then scoop me up and carry me to the top, riding on his shoulders. He'd fly kites for me, holding my arms, showing me how to make the sail dance in the wind. But now he was 'busy with work'. Always busy with work – even at the weekends. He came back when I was in bed and left before I got up or when I was otherwise occupied – in the bathroom or having my breakfast.

When I think back to that last day, I'd like to be able to say that he'd kissed me on the top of the head and called me his 'little chick', then kissed his wife on the cheek and hoped that she had a good day. I'd like to imagine that I'd gone to the window to wave, or stood at the end of the drive, watching his car out of sight, like I did when I was small, but that's not what happened. He just let himself out of the house. We didn't even notice that he'd gone. He got into the car, drove to a wood not very far away and shot himself in the head. I hadn't been enough to keep him alive. Worse than that, I hadn't tried. I'd failed him somehow. If I had shown him how much I cared, then maybe he'd have chosen to go on living. But even worse than that was the feeling I had that he hadn't loved me enough to stay alive. I couldn't get that out of my mind. He'd left me alone to survive on my own. Just her and me.

With him gone, everything was my fault. It was my fault she couldn't go out. If she didn't go out, how was *she going to meet anybody else? With the debts he'd left her, she couldn't even afford a babysitter. She couldn't afford anything. All her friends were going on holiday and she couldn't afford that, either. Even if she could afford it, she'd have to take me with her and what fun would that be? She was too young for this to be happening to her, but what did that matter? Her life was over. He might as well have finished us all off while he was at it.*

Sometimes, I wish he had.

20

I'm not really alive unless I'm with her. I feel as though I've never been fully awake, as if I've been sleepwalking through my life. She makes everything new minted. I think I love her, I really do, but when I try to tell her, she shuts me up, or changes the subject, so I don't know what she thinks, or feels.

I can't figure out where I am with her. I never know exactly where we are going, or what we're going to do, or even if I'm going to see her. She never calls or texts me. She's either there. Or not there. She brings an element of mystery. Something like adventure. She introduces me to new things. Things I've never done before. I can't get enough of her, but she teaches me to wait, to taste and savour; she teaches me the difference between greed and appetite. She likes to be in command.

I don't stop to think what it would be like, how she

would react if things got seriously, and I mean seriously, out of her control; if somebody came along who refused to obey her rules.

'I like to plan things out. Choreograph them,' she says. 'Direct the action.'

'Like a play.'

'More like a film.'

'Is that what you want to do? Make films?'

'No. I want to change the world.'

She is testing me, pushing me, into doing things I wouldn't ordinarily do. Some I don't mind so much. Like having sex in public places.

Some things I do.

'Do it,' she says, 'do it for me. You aren't scared, are you?'

Being scared is not something she understands.

I'm not scared. It's just that this particular thing she wants me to do is betraying a trust. She doesn't understand that, either. I don't think she trusts anybody and doesn't expect anyone to trust her.

She wants me to take a punt out at night, take her down the river. If the boats belonged to anyone else, I wouldn't have a problem. But these are Alan's boats. I know how much they cost. I know how much he worries about theft and vandalism. He's just invested in a heavy-duty chain that runs along the line of them, linking them together, secured by a massive padlock.

I don't say anything, but she senses my reluctance and the reason for it. We are beginning to know what the other one is thinking. At least, she knows what *I'm* thinking. With her, I can never be sure.

'You *care* what he thinks?' She says this like it's a bit of a revelation.

'Yeah. I do.'

She shrugs, like that is an alien concept and gives me a look, like she knows I'll do it anyway, so what's the problem? I'd do anything for her and she knows it, anything she asked me to do.

The chain is shiny and new, some kind of special alloy, impossible to cut through, but I don't need to because I have the key. She stands on the bank, her slim shape dark against the willows and the lights from the town, while I squat in the mud, trying not to drop the key into the water, or fall in myself. I don't want to look nervous, jumpy, but the key slips in my grip a little bit and my hand is shaking slightly as I fit it into the hefty padlock. I'm rubbish at locks at the best of times. My fingers feel banana thick and I wish I'd brought a torch with me. I steady myself and take a breath. The more you think something won't work, the more it isn't going to.

'Having trouble?' Her voice rings down the river, setting the ducks quacking.

I want to shout, 'Shut the fuck up, will you?' But I don't.

I just work away until I hear the key click home. The big hasp comes loose in my hands. The chain slithers down the line of boats as it slackens, rattling in the quiet of the river like machine gun chatter. I sense her impatience like a breath on my neck but I have to be careful to secure the other boats or they could all go floating off down the river and over the weir. She wouldn't care about that – she might even think it was funny – but Alan doesn't deserve that. Plus I have to keep the one I want steady or we'll be going nowhere. Usually, it takes two of us to free the boats.

I'm not even thinking about getting caught or who might be watching, just getting the boat free and ready.

I thought she might act as lookout or even help me. Fat chance. She just stands staring at the river, like she's admiring the play of lights on the water. Like it's nothing to do with her. First sound of a siren, she'd be walking away, leaving me to face the music. Guaranteed. I know it and I don't care. It's a price I'm willing to pay.

When it all looks sorted, she comes down the bank to join me, as nonchalant as if it's Sunday afternoon. I wait, patient as a ferryman, there to serve her. There's no question who's in charge here and I know it. I offer my arm and she smiles as if she sees what I'm thinking. She knows it, too.

I take the pole and guide us out to the middle of the river. The water slips under the till, the black surface rippling with silver, orange, red and green reflected light.

The effect is hypnotic; I try not to look at it, concentrate on what I'm doing. She stares at the patterns sliding by. Once we are away from the bridge, we are out of danger. I relax a bit. The town lights fade from the water, replaced by the matt shadows of the trees, the silver moonlight. From the bank comes the slap and slosh that marks our passage, the secret rustle of small creatures in the undergrowth, the croaking call of a coot in the rushes, the sleepy settle of ducks, huddled together, quacking quietly on a bare patch of bank. We are getting near. The ait is a solid, dark shape in front of us. I can hear the rush and churn of the weir. I take us in under the willows, find the landing point, ship the pole, jump out and tie up. We don't say anything. We just hold hands tightly as we go on to the island.

The willows close behind us, swishing together like ribbon curtains. It's dark inside the tent that the leaves make. I stumble over a root and swear.

'Should have brought a torch.'

'No, she says, 'no torches. I told you before.'

I think that we will stop here, but she leads me on.

'I want to go to the other island,' she says, 'the one across the weir.'

I don't want to do that at all. I find it hard enough in the daytime, let alone at night, but I can't show her that I'm frightened, or even reluctant. She holds my hand tighter and leads me.

Water plunges over the broken lintel, rushing down the

sloping concrete, churning and foaming white above the blackness. The river is deep below the weir, the surface dimpled with eddies and plaited with currents. A branch tumbles over and does not reappear.

She skips across. I stand and watch her. I should just do it. Don't think. I can hear Rob's voice in my head. *Just do it. You think too much.* She beckons, calling me on. I step out. Halfway across, a stone rocks and nearly tips me down on to the concrete weir. It's always the same one but this time it's even further out of position, right over the edge. I nearly lose my balance and seesaw backwards and forwards, the dark water flowing past my feet so fast that it looks glossy and solid, like glass. It hisses with the speed of its falling, seething white and frothing at the bottom of the concrete slope. I see the branch bob up again, turned and tossed like a twig in the white water. How long was it under there being tumbled over and over? One minute? Two minutes? Long enough to drown.

'Come on. Quickly,' she calls to me. 'Do it quickly. Look at me.' She holds her hand out, crossing back for me, the water flowing fast over and round her bare feet. 'Don't look down.'

Our hands don't meet, but it's as if there is an invisible rope joining us. She steps backwards as I move forwards. She gains the bank and suddenly I'm there beside her. I don't mean to but I nearly push her over, we both stagger back, falling on to a soft bed of silvery leaves. I lie there, shivering and sweating. She sits with her hands clasped round her knees. In the moonlight, her face is washed of colour.

'Fear death by water,' she whispers. Her eyes are huge and black as the river. 'It was in the rune cast. On the windowsill where you let the stones fall. I noticed it after you left. What if I turn a tarot card, what will I find?' She says quietly, almost to herself. 'The Drowned Phoenician Sailor?' She leans forward, her hair swinging like a curtain. 'The card that is blank. It is something he carries on his back.' She looks up at me. '*Your* card, Jamie.'

She's acting so strange that I feel a different kind of chill, the short hairs rising. 'Do you believe all that?'

'Not me, stupid! T.S. Eliot.'

As if to defy the words she's just spoken, she takes off her dress, walks back on to the slippery stones and steps straight off into the pool behind the weir where the river is deep and still. She disappears for heart-stopping seconds, then breaks the surface, sending out silver ripples.

'You can't swim here!' I stand up and shout down at her. 'There are signs up all over the place!'

The water's got to be full of all kinds of crap, you could catch anything from it, and the bottom could be littered with all sorts of stuff: broken bottles, old crates, supermarket trolleys. She ignores me. For her, prohibition acts as some kind of permission. Rules are there to be broken. She swims out and turns, treading water, laughing at me, beckoning like some kind of dangerous water spirit.

I strip off and jump in, just to show her. I swim out a

little bit and then back again. I'm careful not to swallow any water.

'You look like a mermaid,' I say as she pulls her self out of the pool.

'You mean lorelei or nixie. Mermaids belong to the sea.'

'It's dangerous to swim here.'

'Water's my element. It won't harm me.'

She lays a towel down on top of the blanket that she has brought with her. Her skin is mushroom cool and her hair smells of the river. She pulls me to her. I hear distant sounds: a shout of male laughter, a high yelping scream, a siren's wail.

On the way back, I'm extra careful crossing the weir. Looks to me like someone has shifted the stone in the middle, the one that's loose. It's right out of place, set at an angle. It would take the full force of the river in spate to shift it that much. Someone must have moved it. Why would you do that?

We don't go to the island at night again.

21

I thought I'd throw in a little bit of scare – I knew she was planning to take him there. She likes a thrill. Midnight boating – moonlight trips to the island. Real romantic. Mind if I puke. She's special – I'm not sure he deserves her. I know which one will go arse over tip down the weir and it ain't gonna be her – ha fucking ha.

Her and me – we got stuff in common. You wouldn't think it but we do. Not just the obvious.

Below the surface stuff.

I was out at her place the other night – we talked a long time. She was telling me about her dad and what happened to him and pretty soon I'm telling her about mine.

Jimbo was a little kid when it happened. The old man left him alone mostly – when it was bad I'd get him to hide in the wardrobe – make it a game like. Don't know if he remembers that. Then he weren't around any more and Jim wanted to know about him so I'd tell him stories – adventures with Dad as the hero. I ain't much good at making things up so I lifted stuff from films – Andy McNab – whatever. Jim sucked it all in – eyes wide. He wanted a hero so I gave him one.

Kids need heroes – especially ones who will be growing up without a dad. Maybe I wanted one, too.

It weren't like that in real life.

Truth was he could be a right bastard. OK one minute and next he'd be off on one. Short Fuse.

When he come home – it was like Christmas and birthday rolled together – presents and everything. All good. But after a bit he'd get edgy – restless – then he'd start drinking. If Ma said anything – he'd clip her one and go out and not come back for hours – sometimes days.

One time he bought me a Buzz Lightyear – two days later he'd stomped on old Buzz. Getting On His Nerves. Me? Buzz? Could have been either one of us. He bought me another one but it weren't the same.

You never knew where you were with him. I learnt to wait for the sun to come out and I learnt to keep out of the way.

Now I can see how it was with him. He didn't mean to be harsh. Just couldn't help it. I've seen it in other guys – seen it in myself.

Mum told us Dad's death was an accident. Killed in

training using live rounds. She's always stuck to that story. Truth was he topped himself. Grandpa told me when he'd had one too many whiskies and his marbles were sliding. Went like this:

HIM: You got the look of him.

ME: Oh, who's that?

HIM: Yer dad.

Then nothing. No point prompting you just had to go with him – following the riffs of his mind.

HIM: He were a nasty piece of work. Treated yer mum like dirt. It were worse after that do in Suez.

ME: He weren't in Suez, Grandpa.

HIM: He were out there somewhere.

ME: It was the Gulf War.

HIM: Same difference, int it?

ME: He had Gulf War Syndrome.

HIM: Syndrome my arse. We seen far worse than them lot and didn't behave like that.

ME: Could've been post-traumatic stress disorder – that's what they say I've got.

HIM: Yeah but you been in some real fighting not fannying about in Germany and Northern Ireland.

ME: Northern Ireland was no picnic.

HIM: Not when I were there maybe with the paras – but they was just peacekeeping – never did nothing. He were a coward, lad. Took the coward's way out.

ME: How do you mean? His death was an accident.

HIM: Accident with live rounds – that's what they

always say to cover it up. He topped hisself pure and simple. I'm off to bed.

Fighting – killing – does damage. Grandpa says it's the coward's way out but I don't agree. I bet even he's thought about it. I've been tempted and I know I ain't the only one.

No mistakes with a gun in your mouth. That's no cry for help – just a mess for someone to clear up.

No one gets away free – not me – not Dad – not Grandpa. He can say what he likes. He don't do terms like syndrome – disorder – but they're just names for things he'd rather not talk about. I bet he gave Gran a hard time sometimes. He had his black moods when they all had to tiptoe round him – Mum told me. He's always preferred his mates or why was he forever down the Legion? He's always liked a drink or three. Sometimes even your mates are too much and you have to be on your own. He knows that – else why'd he spend so much time down the allotment and going fishing?

Death is the end of the road – the ultimate destination where you can be alone. Maybe that's what Dad figured out – it was the only place left to go.

Jamie still don't know what really happened to Dad. I told her not to tell him.

We talked all night. In her own way she's as fucked as I am. I told her things I've never told no one. I never felt that close to anyone – not even Bryn or the other guys. Sure, you'd die for them – them for you – that's a

www.urflixstar.com/robvid

given – but you never talk about deep stuff – personal stuff – about your dad and from when you were a kid and that, for fear of looking weak and them taking the piss.

She makes me feel real – it's painful – like blood pumping back into a limb that's been kept immobile but she makes me feel like I'm coming alive.

She says she don't do love. I don't neither – but she's the nearest I've got to it.

22

She doesn't say anything about where we are going. I might as well be blindfolded. I catch the sweetish scent of alcohol on her breath as we wait on the bridge for the temporary lights to change.

'Have you been drinking?'

'Might have been.'

'You shouldn't drink and drive.'

'No shit!' She shakes her head. 'I didn't know that. Thanks for telling me.'

I settle back in my seat and hope we don't have far to go. Nothing happens. There are no police sirens. She drives more carefully, if anything, but I'm relieved when she takes the turning into the Meadow Crofts development and I know we are going to her place.

She has a bottle ready on a tray, together with lime and salt.

'I don't like tequila,' I say.

'It's *not* tequila,' she says. 'It's *mescal*.' She shows me the scorpion in the bottom of the bottle, shaking it, making it float about, like it's swimming in there. 'It is the best and only the best is good enough. Drink up.'

We are sitting on the floor in the living room. I pass on the next round but she pours herself another. And another. She puts down the bottle, nearly missing the edge of the smoked-glass table. She did have a bit of a head start, but she seems to be getting really pissed. More than I've ever seen her. Mescal is strong stuff. She doesn't slur her words. The way she speaks, all her movements become slower, more deliberate, and she's very careful, like she doesn't like to lose control. She never talks about her past, other boys, the men she's had. She rarely talks about herself at all. The less she says, the more I want to know about her. I decide now's my opportunity.

I go into the kitchen to get a beer, play for time, think about how to approach her.

The fridge is stacked with champagne bottles and the table is covered with shopping bags, the glossy, expensive kind, like she's just come back from a spending spree.

I turn to find her standing in the doorway.

'That one is for you.' She points to a dark green bag, marked Ralph Lauren. 'It's a shirt to replace the one you spilt ketchup down. I had to guess the size.'

I take the shirt out of the packing. It's a pink and white

striped button down. Not what I'd wear normally, but I'm touched that she thought of me.

'Hey, thanks!'

'Try it on.'

'Now?' I follow her back into the lounge.

'Of course, now. No point in buying things if you aren't going to wear them.'

I do as she says. It fits perfectly.

'Let me see,' she says, moving me round like I'm a mannequin. 'Looks good.'

'How come you can afford all this?' I ask her as I finish buttoning the shirt.

'She left me money and Trevor gave me more. Plus I've got a credit card.'

'What about your dad? Do you ever see him?'

'My dad, my real dad, the one who is not called Trevor? No. I don't see him because he's dead. He shot himself,' she says after a pause. 'We have that much in common.'

I choke on my beer. 'What do you mean?'

'What I said. He's dead.'

'No, not that.' I put the bottle down. 'What you said about my dad. Having that in common. My dad was killed in an accident. He was a soldier, out on exercise. They were using live rounds. It was an *accident*,' I repeat. 'What makes you think it wasn't?'

'I dunno. I just thought. . .' Her eyes are unfocused, distracted. All that mescal is getting to her. 'Maybe it was something Martha said –'

'But it's not true, so why should she say it?'

'I don't know.' She tips the bottle. 'Almost empty.'

She gets up to go and get more, but I pull her back down again.

'No.' I take the bottle from her. 'Not until you tell me. How do you know?'

She pulls away and goes to the kitchen.

She comes back with another bottle 'Want some?' I shake my head. 'Please yourself.' She pours herself a shot and knocks it back. 'Dead's dead. You just have to accept it. My dad went out one day and never came back. He got into the car, drove to a wood and shot himself.'

She's quiet, staring into space, as if revisiting that time, going back to that place.

'That's terrible,' I say into the silence. 'A terrible thing to happen but that's not what happened to my dad. His was an accident.'

'Oh,' she looks at me, eyes heavy. 'How do you know?'

'It's what I was told.'

'How old were you?'

'Not very old. Three.'

'There!' She sits up. 'You've got it right there. They lied to you. They'd have lied to me, too, if I hadn't been old enough to see through it. People don't like the truth. They translate it into something easier for everyone to accept.'

My turn to be quiet. Everything I'd ever believed. Everything I'd ever been told. She's rocking my world. I reach for the mescal bottle and take a swig. Little things come together in my mind. A word here, a word there. Hushed conversations I wasn't supposed to hear. The more I think about it, the more I know what she is saying is true.

Just when I think it can't get worse, it does.

'But how do you know?' I ask. 'When it's something I didn't know myself. How do you know?' It can't be from Martha. I'm pretty sure she knows as much as I do.

'It was Rob,' she says it quickly, as if she wants to get this over. 'Rob told me.'

'But how . . .'

'There's something you ought to know.'

Then she tells me what really happened at Martha's party.

I leave in the cold, early morning. I don't know if it's the mescal, or what she's told me, but my face feels stiff, like a mask. I feel disarticulated, as if my arms and legs don't belong to my body. I can't feel my feet but I manage to put one in front of the other. I've got plenty to think about on the long walk home.

23

'If I can't dance, I don't want to be part of your
revolution.'
Attrib. Emma Goldman

I don't know if Emma G really said it, but I hope she did.

He's right. I shouldn't drink. Never mind the driving bit. I can't keep track of what I'm saying. Why did I tell him about his dad? I promised Rob I wouldn't. It just slipped out. I certainly shouldn't drink mescal; it acts like a truth drug. I was wrecked and reckless, or I never would have told him. Or what happened at Martha's birthday. Despite reports to the contrary, I'm not that much of a bitch.

He's perceptive. He knew I'd been lying about the party. He just didn't know why. Of course I remember.

I felt out of place. Had done all night. I was new to the school. My friendship with Martha had happened quickly (she's like that, given to sudden enthusiasms for people) and developed with an intensity that bewildered me. I should have been more wary. I was nearly a year younger than her, even though we were in the same year group. Her friends didn't like me for taking her away from them and I didn't really fit in.

It was all dependent on Martha. If she'd been on my side, it would have been OK, but she wasn't. That's the other thing about her, she can turn for no reason. All it takes is some slight, real or imagined, and she's not your friend any more. Bad time for it to happen. During the evening, I felt her turning against me, siding with the others. As soon as they saw this, they were on me like a pack of dogs. From my choice of pizza topping, to the clothes I was wearing, everything I did, everything I said, was wrong and open to ridicule. Martha didn't join in – she just sat back and watched, enjoying the power she had over them – and me. I'd have gone, but I didn't want them to know how much they were getting to me and I didn't want to upset her mum who'd gone to a lot of trouble. I escaped to her bedroom, joining the ones who'd had too much of the spiked Fanta. I figured I'd rather be puked on than take the outpouring of vitriol down in the living room. I'd just stay there. Wait it out.

It looked like it was going to be a long night. One, two, three o'clock in the morning. I heard Martha's mum go down and have a word, turn off the TV. I pretended to be asleep as Martha came in to claim her bed. The others had to find somewhere to crash on the floor. I couldn't sleep. The more I thought about it, the worse it got. It wasn't just the stuffiness that got me, the proximity of bodies. It was their hostility. The room was crowded, but there was a *cordon sanitaire* around me. The latecomers had stumbled in, whispering, giggling, taking exaggerated care not to set their sleeping bags near to me. I felt trapped. My sleeping bag binding round me like a nylon coffin. I was choking back tears as I lay there, eyes open, with the darkness beginning to take on substance, weighing down on me, clogging my nose and mouth like black cotton wool. I couldn't breathe. I didn't want to disturb the others, but I knew I couldn't stay there. I had to get up.

It was easier than I thought. Once I was standing, the panic left me. The darkness seemed less total. I could see a path through the bodies to the door. As soon as I was out of the room, I began to feel better. The air was cool. There was light from the street outside. I remembered where the bathroom was. Second door on the right. I crept down the corridor, not wanting to wake any of the family.

I didn't know what the time was, but I guessed it must be getting towards morning. I thought everybody but me was asleep, but a light showed from the room at the end of the hall. I don't know why I did it, but I glided past the bathroom and went to look through the crack in the door.

Rob was lying on the bed. I don't know how old he was. Seventeen? Eighteen? He was back from his first tour. He was more man than boy now. It was a hot night and there was a sheen over his skin; the muscles showed: curved and shadowed, like sculpture. He was wearing briefs, but he might as well have been naked. I was transfixed.

He must have heard me – sensed me, anyway. He didn't say anything but he got off the bed. I just stood there as he padded over and opened the door. He invited me into his room.

'Can't sleep?'

I didn't say anything. I just stood there.

'Me neither. It's the heat. Want some of this?' He offered me cider that he had down by the side of the bed. I shook my head.

'What's the matter? Cat got your tongue? You don't have to talk if you don't want to. Have you been crying?' He wiped a tear from my cheek with his thumb. 'Come here.'

He put his arms round me. He'd just had a shower. His hair was still wet. He smelt of mint and marshmallow. His skin felt smooth. He kissed me then. His mouth hard on mine. I'd never even been kissed before, not like this, anyway – by someone who knew what he was doing. Before I knew it, we were on the bed. He pushed my hair back from my face and smiled. Then he peeled off my top. I didn't even try to stop him. I was curious. Curious to know all the things I'd heard hinted at, whispered about. If I was a novice, he was not. The most surprising thing was I liked it. The kissing and caressing made me feel things that I had never felt before, made me feel special and powerful. In the way that girls calculated such things then, I went from zero to ten.

Afterwards, he asked me if I was all right.

'Yes,' I said. 'Fine.'

It was my first time. I didn't want him to know that, but I'm sure he guessed. I just lay there next to him. I remember feeling released. I'd done it. I didn't need to wonder what it was like any more. I had to get out of the room without anyone knowing. The worst thing, the very worst thing, would be for them all to know what had happened.

I slid off the bed and left him, let myself out quietly, still worried about waking people. As soon as I was out of the room, the shock of what had happened hit me like a cold blast of air. I had to steady myself against the wall. Above all else, above every other consideration, I did not want anyone to know.

Fat chance of that. Martha saw me. She was waiting for me when I came out of his room. I could see in her eyes that she knew. I went to push past her. She put her arm up to stop me.

'Don't think you can go back there like nothing has happened.' She hissed the words close to my ear. 'Get out, you little slag.'

She threw my stuff down the stairs by way of encouragement and I left, walking through the night. Martha's mum must have phoned mine. She drove out and found me.

She was annoyed.

'What's the matter with you? What made you walk out like that?'

I wasn't going to tell her, so I said nothing.

In the face of my silence, she filled the air between us with complaints, about me. I wasn't normal, how could I be? What was I doing, walking out of somebody's house in the middle of the night? What would people think? That girl's poor mother must have been beside herself. You hear such terrible stories. I was so selfish. Never thought about anyone else. Never thought about consequences. No wonder I didn't have any friends. Didn't I have anything to say?

I shook my head and stared out of the window.

I took after my father; he'd always been a loner. Always the same. The silent treatment. Didn't I have a tongue in my head? If I wasn't careful, I'd be going the same way. He'd ruined her life. She wasn't about to let me do the same. Didn't I want her to be happy? Why didn't I think about her for a change?

As if I ever had the chance to do anything else.

Didn't I want some security for both of us? Didn't I want us to be part of a proper family? I could see where this was going. She was talking about Trevor. They weren't married then.

Did I think she could go on for ever, doing everything? Did I think one income was enough? She was still a young woman (well, comparatively). Didn't she deserve a bit of companionship?

I let her follow the well-worn grooves of her complaints against me, against life in general and the hand it had dealt her. Everything was my fault. I'd ruined her life just by being born. That was when it all began to go wrong. Everything was fine before that. Perfect, in fact. I was a mistake.

She used to go on about that in her rows with Dad.

I wasn't really listening. I'd heard it all before. I wore the guilt like a pinching shoe. You can get used to anything in time.

Not long after that the whispers started, the messages, notes passed around, magic marker in the toilets, at the bus stop.

Vanessa Carington is A SLAG

What do I care? It wasn't me up there. They couldn't even spell my name correctly. Martha was behind it, I'm pretty sure of that, although she never said anything to my face. She sowed the seeds. No one ever knew what I'd done, or who I'd been with, to earn the sobriquet, but then nobody cared. Gossip creates its own reality. I am a slag because everyone says I am. Impossible to defend yourself against that, so I didn't bother. It amused me that people called me that but didn't know exactly why. That was not the reaction Martha expected. The campaign intensified. It didn't work, because I simply didn't care.

When I told Jamie, he lied and said it didn't matter. I didn't know whether to love or despise him for that. I ought to finish with him. Now. Stop dragging it out. It seems like every time I see him, I hurt him. He doesn't deserve that. I still haven't told him everything. That would finish it for good and I need him. He's my lodestone, the compass that points me towards normal. I'm not ready to let him go. I want to make it up to him, so I begin downloading music: The Vaccines, Arcade Fire, Cold War Kids, Friendly Fires, Crystal Castles, along with older stuff: Libertines, Smiths, Stone Roses. The kind of thing I think he will like.

What I didn't tell him is that Rob and I went on seeing each other. He was there one day outside school, waiting for Martha. He had a car and was supposed to take her somewhere. He went home with me. We began meeting. In secret. He had a girlfriend back then so it was all very clandestine. The secrecy made it doubly exciting. We'd hook up when he was home on leave. I'd get a text and meet him. We'd go somewhere no one would see us, like the allotment shed or al fresco out on the ait. Sometimes a cheap motel on the ring road or off the motorway.

When he was away, he used to send me stuff. Video diaries. He's not one for writing. The early ones were funny – montages spliced together with a soldier's blunt, black humour. They got progressively less humorous until they were harrowing. Brutal as a bayonet.

And then I didn't hear from him any more. I only knew he was home because of Martha. She'd begun Avon

Against the War by that time. How they trembled in Whitehall and Washington. She organised petitions, went on demonstrations. I joined just to piss her off. There was nothing she could do about it. Societies were open to any member of the school body. Some of the staff were doubtful about the politics (they do tend to the conservative) but they were keen on anything that would encourage the girls to think about something other than boys, going out, MTV and vacuous TV series.

Rob was her prime exhibit. Look what's happened to my brother. His leg's shattered, he has post-traumatic stress disorder. He might never *be normal.*

I'd smile to myself. Who said he was normal in the first place? Then I'd think about how he'd react if he knew she'd told the whole school about him.

He *won't be returning to the front line, but others will, she'd say, fixing us with her steely gaze. Boys like him. To brutalise and be brutalised in turn on war's eternal carousel.*

She's right about that but petitions and peaceful protests aren't going to change a thing. No one cares. Even Martha has moved on to other causes: eco issues, wind farms, carbon footprint. They must be made to care.

The front line is always somewhere else. Never here.

But it's getting closer.

Time to bring it right back home.

24

I don't hear from her. It's because of the thing she told me. Has to be. I want to tell her it doesn't matter, but I can't text her or call her because I haven't got her number. I jump every time I hear my phone's ringtone or the buzz of an incoming message. I sleep with the phone right next to me in case she calls in the middle of the night, in case she messages me. I'm on it before the first ring ends, just as it begins to buzz, but it's never her. It's always Cal or one of my other friends. As soon as I see who it is, I shut off the call and don't answer.

I'm in agony thinking that she must have finished with me.

I don't go round to her house to try to see her. I tell myself that it's because she wouldn't like it, but really it's because I'm afraid of who I'll meet.

I can't sleep. I begin to get up super early and ride out

on my bike, or just walk. You hit countryside about a hundred metres from our house. There are paths out across the fields, down to the river. I wonder what it would be like to keep walking and never go back. I wave to a guy out on a tractor. He waves back. The next day the wheat field is all stubble. The summer is turning.

Sometimes, I take the path down to the river and return through town. I see people walking to work: office workers, girls with summer jobs in the shops. Work on the bridge is still snarling up the traffic. Drivers sweating in shirtsleeves, swearing, talking on their mobiles. One day, I see Rob coming out of the multi-storey car park that's being redeveloped. He's wearing workman's clothes and has got a bag with him. I wonder if he's got a job there. It's been boarded up for ages. According to the local paper the developers ran out of money. It's turned into a bit of an eyesore. Maybe they are starting on the demolition. I don't go near him and he doesn't see me.

Just when I'm certain that I've been dumped, I get a message. She's picking me up tonight.

Martha's back from Cornwall and she's going out, so I'm playing bathroom guerrilla warfare again. When I hear her going to her bedroom to get something, I'm straight in there.

'Hey! I haven't finished yet!'

'You have now!'

I lock the door while she hammers and fumes and calls for Mum like we were little kids again. Eventually she goes away and I carry on shaving. I like shaving. I like the ritual. Rob taught me like Grandpa taught him. We use a brush and soap, not that squirty stuff. I have to hide my razor so that Martha doesn't use it to shave her legs.

I smooth my chin. No nicks. Pretty good job.

'All yours now.'

'About time.' She comes out of her room. 'I hate to think what you're doing in there.'

'Shaving. It's something men do.'

'I'm amazed you need to.' She sniffs. 'Grown-up after-shave, eh? Lynx not good enough for her? I take it she's the lucky lady.'

'Might be.'

She shakes her head. 'I can't believe you're still seeing her. I'd have thought she'd have dumped you weeks ago.'

'Well, she hasn't. Now if you'll excuse me, I have to get ready.'

I think she'll take this opportunity to move into the bathroom, but she doesn't.

'Going to her place? Don't start getting ideas above your station.' She makes a face. 'Those houses are *soooo* naff. Talk about conspicuous consumption.' She looks through the door into our shared facilities, lip curling. 'I bet *she's* got an en suite, and everything. No expense spared.'

'You're right there. She has, with marble basins and gold taps.'

'Really?'

'No. I lied about the gold taps.'

She follows me into my room.

'Do you mind?' I look down. I'm only wearing a towel.

'I can't *believe* you are still seeing her.'

'You've said that once.'

'You ought to find someone more . . . suitable. Lee really likes you,' she says, sitting on the end of my bed. You'd be better off with her.'

'Lee's a nice girl,' I say, non-committal. That's not going to happen. It would be like trading in a Harley-Davidson for a trail bike. 'What do you care who I go out with?'

'I *do* care. I care about you.'

I laugh. 'Since when?'

'You're my *brother*. I don't want to see you get hurt.'

'Double ha, ha.'

I know from the signs that she's got something else on her mind. I take some product and start working it into my hair.

'She's seeing someone else.'

I don't stop messing with my hair, even for a second, but I feel suddenly numb inside, like I've swallowed a chunk of ice and it's lodged somewhere near my heart.

I keep staring into the mirror, making sure Martha's eyes meet mine.

'If this is a wind-up, or gossip from your bitchy friends, I'll kill you. And them.'

She shakes her head. 'Lee said it and she's not like that.

She says she's seeing someone.'

'I never said we were exclusive.' I try to make out I'm completely unfazed. 'Who is it, anyway? Not the Art teacher. I know about him.'

'No,' she shakes her head. 'Not Charlie Hands.'

'How does Lee know?'

'She lives near her. She was taking the dog for a walk, or something, and saw him leaving.'

'I didn't know she had a dog.'

'Well, she does.'

'Does she take it for a walk every morning?'

'How would I know? How's that the point? She saw someone leaving Caro's and –'

'It could have been me leaving,' I say.

'That's what she thought. At first. You look kind of similar.' She looks at me. 'Especially from a distance.'

Everyone says how much I look like my brother. That is the killer shot.

'I mean, she couldn't be *certain*, but . . . I just thought you ought to know, that's all.' She's drifting towards the door now. 'I hope you haven't been using my shampoo. I told you about that before.'

I hear the sound of Caro's car but I can't make myself hurry. I check my pockets: keys, phone, wallet. The numbness is spreading through me, making it impossible to move quickly.

I get into the car.

'You took your time.'

I shrug.

'What's the matter?'

'Nothing.'

'Good.' She smiles. 'Because I've got a surprise for you.'

'Fine,' I say.

She starts the car, then kills the engine.

'What's up?'

'Nothing, I told you.'

'Yes, there is. Tell me.'

'Nothing. Like I said.'

I'd got in the car thinking of ways to confront her, but when it comes to it, I can't think how to do it, can't think what to say.

'We'll stay here, then.' She puts both hands on the wheel.

'It's, well, it's something Martha said.'

'Martha, eh?' She drums her fingers. She's wearing red nail varnish. 'And what did Martha say?'

'She said you were seeing someone. Someone else.'

'Did she say who this *someone* might be?'

'Well, not specifically. It was more of a hint.'

'I see. And what was she hinting at?'

'She was hinting that it might be Rob.'

She's quiet for a moment, taking in the information. 'Where did she hear that?'

'Lee told her.'

She nods her head slowly, taking in what I'm telling her.

'So, you got this from Martha, who hates me, and sad little Lee who desperately wants to be her friend while equally desperately fancying you. I see. Impartial sources, both of them.'

'If you put it like that . . .'

She's offering me a get out and I'm quick to accept it.

'Who's it to be? Them or me?'

She starts the car but leaves the engine idling. Deep inside, I know what Martha says could be true but against my better judgement, against all my instincts, I choose her. Besides, what was I going to do? Where would I go? Back home to a gloating Martha? Out to see Cal and my mates, all of them saying, 'I told you so'? I stay put. I don't get out of the car.

She doesn't say anything. Doesn't even look at me. Just drives off.

I don't ask her anything more, just listen to the music. The playlist is all bands I like. I look over at her.

'Did you do this for me?'

'Who else?' She doesn't take her eyes off the road. 'Not exactly my kind of thing.'

'Hey, thanks!' I don't know what else to say.

'My pleasure,' she says. Then she smiles at me.

After that, I don't care where we are going. I just want to drive. Sometimes that's enough. I don't like to arrive. I refuse to think about what Martha told me. I keep pushing it out of my mind. Right now, there's just her and me going into the dark tunnel of the night, lit only by the headlights. I don't want to think about anything. I glance over to steal a look at her profile, at the way the hair curls by her ear, the curve of her neck, how the muscles move under her skin every time she turns the wheel or changes gear. She's wearing the spotted dress I like and thin silver bracelets on her arms. They slip and slide up and down as she drives. I'm too absorbed to take in our direction. Then we are on the motorway.

'Nowhere local, then?'

'We're going to the seaside,' she says, and laughs.

The nearest sea is at least a hundred miles away, but I'm not arguing. We stop at an all-night services for petrol and to drink coffee to keep awake. After that it's through the night. I fall asleep and fight it and fall asleep again. I dream that we're racing down a steep hill on bicycles. Her, me and a guy I can't see. We're abreast of each other. The road in front has collapsed. Wooden barriers block off a deep, dark chasm. None of us can stop.

I jerk awake just as I crash through the barriers and over the edge. I apologise for sleeping while she's driving.

'You were snoring. And drooling.'

I wipe my chin and swig some water. Offer her some. She takes the bottle off me and sips it.

'Thanks.'

'No problem. Are we nearly there yet?' I sound like a kid going on holiday.

'About eighty miles.'

I fall asleep again and when I next wake up I'm shivering. It's early morning and we are there.

I know the place.

'We used to come here when we were kids,' I say. 'Cal and I came camping last year.'

It was a good laugh. After GCSEs. Down on the beach, every night was party night. I met a girl called Nia. She lived up here. I really liked her. I messaged her all the way home and was on Facebook every night. We made plans to meet but after a bit she stopped messaging me. Her Facebook page showed her down on the beach with some other guy. The next week, there she was with another. The party was still going on for her without me.

I start telling Caro about it as she drives down to the harbour front, but she's not really interested.

'Hang on a sec.'

She gets out of the car and disappears. She comes back with coffee and bacon rolls.

'There's a stall down by the quay where the fishing boats come in.'

She takes a bite of her roll, sauce and grease oozing down her chin. She's obviously been here before, too, but doesn't seem inclined to share her experiences. We sit and watch as the night fades and the day comes on. The sea gives off a sequin glitter as the first light ripples over it. When the town is coming to life, she starts the car.

'Where are we going now?'

'Beach further down the coast.'

She drives past the main beach with its campsite sprawl

of bright nomad tents, and takes a winding track to a little bay. The inlet is still in shadow, although the far headland is lit by the sun. There are tents dotted around in the dunes but it's still very early and they are all firmly zipped up. She strips off her dress and runs down the beach, diving straight into the breaking waves. She's a powerful swimmer. She swims crawl with long, strong strokes until her head is a dot breaking through waves like a seal. I strip off and follow her. The water is freezing. Not even OK when you get used to it. I only stay in a couple of minutes.

I stand by the car and shiver in my wet Calvins while I wait for her to get out.

'There are towels in the boot.'

I drape one round her and begin to rub her dry. She does the same for me. I'm still cold, can't stop shivering. We grab our clothes and she leads me into the dunes, away from the tents and the sparse scattering of cars. We find a place and she spreads the blanket for us. She offers me brandy from a silver flask and puts her arms around me, pulling me to her. I feel the fiery spirit spreading through me and I am no longer cold.

Afterwards, we dress and climb to the top of the nearest dune and sit looking out at the sea. The sand is cool, silky to the touch. I sift the grains through my fingers. The beach is just one monochrome, but each grain is different in shape and colour. How many are there? Even here, running through my hands? I take a handful of sand and let it trickle down on to her foot, half burying it. She wriggles her toes, letting it sink further. She's wearing that thin gold chain round her ankle. On the inside, below the bone, there are those lines that I noticed before. I can see them better now. Striations, straight little white marks, slightly raised, scored across the skin. She notices me noticing.

'I used to cut myself.' She says it like that. Completely matter of fact. 'It's a place people don't notice. I used to do it here, too.' She pushes the thin silver bracelets up her arm to show the inside of her wrist. 'I did it with a razor blade. The old-fashioned kind. They are the best. Quick cut.' She grips finger and thumb together, as though holding the blade, and makes a quick cutting motion. 'Doesn't hurt. Well, not much. Like a paper cut.'

'But why? Why would you do something like that?'

'I used to like to see the blood.'

I don't say anything, just think how much hurt she must have felt to make her want to harm herself. The scars are like a bar code, the little lines containing the key to the self she wants to hide. She puts her hand to the place, as if to shield it from my gaze.

'It makes you feel better,' she says. 'Lets out the pressure. It's no big deal.'

I shake my head. It *is* a big deal to me.

'Do you do it now?' I ask.

'No,' she shakes her head. 'I don't do it any more.'

That doesn't mean that the hurt has gone. I want to hold her, make her understand that I want to take some of that pain away, but I'm not sure how she'd take it. I don't want her to think I feel sorry for her, she'd hate that. I hesitate just too long. The camp is stirring. A man emerges from one of the tents and the moment is lost.

The guy's tanned a dark brown, like he's been there all summer. He's wearing flip-flops and an old, faded pair of raggedy cut-offs. His hair is long, tawny from the sea and sun. He stands for a moment, taking in the morning. Then he sees us. He waves and comes over.

'Hi, Caro. Nice to see you.' He smiles at her but when he looks at me his expression hardens just a little. 'And this is?'

'This is Jamie,' she says. 'He's a friend.'

'Hi, Jamie. I'm Theo.'

He puts out his hand but his look stays hard and appraising, his smile doesn't get near his eyes. He's older than I first thought. His hair is streaked with grey and thinning. The stubble lining his jaw is like a dusting of iron filings.

'I haven't seen you before, have I?'

I shake my head.

'Welcome,' he says, but I don't think he means it.

He leads us over to where a woman has got a fire going. She has a couple of kids with her and a mongrel dog. Her fair hair is in long braids and she is wearing a brightly coloured wrap-around dress like one Mum brought back from her trip to Thailand. She throws some bacon and sausages in a pan. The smell brings other people out of their tents.

'You hungry? Molly will give you something to eat,' Theo says to me. 'Caro and I have got some catching up to do.' He turns to Caro. 'Let's walk.'

It's pretty clear I'm not invited.

'You nearly missed us,' he's saying. 'Business in other places. We need to be where it's happening. This could be it, you know, Caro . . .'

They move out of earshot.

'How's it going, Molly? I'm starving.' A tall guy in a vest and baggy pirate pants comes over to join us at the fire.

'Be ready in a bit.' The woman shakes the pan.

'Hi,' he says to me. 'I'm Paul.' He squints down at me. 'You been here before?'

I shake my head.

He looks at me closely for a second, then shrugs. 'I just thought – maybe I've seen you somewhere else.'

'Could be,' I say, although I doubt it. 'Maybe you're mixing me up with somebody.'

I don't want to think about who that might be.

'Have you been to Dean Street with Caro?' Molly asks. They are both looking at me now.

I shake my head. I know the place but make no comment. All my friends think they're druggies and dropouts.

'Whatever. You're welcome.' Paul squats down and shakes my hand.

'Here, these look just about ready.' Molly forks a piece

of blackened bacon and a sausage into a roll and offers it over to me.

I take a bite. The sausage is pink in the middle and the roll is stale.

'We forage,' she says, by way of excuse or explanation. 'Practise freegonomics. The supermarkets throw so much away. Another sausage?'

'Nah, I'm good.' I smile at her and look for ways to feed my breakfast to the dog.

'I will, Moll. Thanks.' Paul isn't so fussy. He helps himself to another of Tesco's *Finest*. 'Want coffee?'

'Yeah. Thanks.'

Molly pours some brew into a tin mug. The coffee is better than the food but I just want to go.

I have to wait for Caro. I can see them down the beach. They've stopped walking. Caro is drawing with a stick on the sand. She looks up at the Theo guy, brow furrowed. When she's talking, she has a tendency to use her hands. She's gesticulating, describing words in the air. He's nodding. He's listening, paying attention to what she's saying. Then it's his turn to talk, hers to listen. They turn back and walk towards us, still deep in conversation. He glances up suddenly and catches me watching. He looks at me suspiciously as if I'm some kind of spy. He says something to Caro. Her laugh, high and clear, carries way up the beach.

'Thanks for the advice,' she says as he delivers her back.

'No problem. I'll let you know where to find us. Good luck, Caro.'

He embraces her, then holds her away from him for a second. There's no secret sign or anything, but something passes between them, something I'm missing.

'How do you know them?' I ask as we walk back to the car.

'Oh, going on demos. Actions. You get to meet people.'

'And who is Theo exactly?'

'He's like their leader. They lived in a house down on Dean Street. I used to hang out there. They've come here for the summer.'

'So you've been here before?'

'A couple of times.'

'Who did you come with?'

She frowns, as if trying to think. 'Charlie came with me once. He's friends with Theo and he wanted to take photos of the old pier.'

Charlie Hands doesn't look anything like me, that's for sure, but I don't say anything.

'I admire them,' she's saying. 'They are committed. To a cause.'

'Oh, what would that be?'

'They want change – big change. *Global* change. And they are prepared to take action to get it.'

'Lots of people want change.'

'Yes, but they aren't prepared to *do* anything. They aren't prepared to act. They're too scared. They don't want their lives to be affected. They are too frightened of losing what they have got. They aren't prepared to make the sacrifice, take it to the limit.'

'And you are?'

'Yes. I am. I mean, what have I got to lose?'

'A lot.'

'Like what?'

'You're great-looking, brainy, young, your whole life in front of you.'

'Yeah? Oh, yeah?' Her eyes are dark and wild. They make me think of razor blades, bar-code scars. 'Well, I don't see it that way.'

'Why don't you join them if you feel so strongly,' I say, although I can't see her living like this, scrounging up food out of supermarket skips.

'I don't do camping. I told you before. There are lots of different roles for people to take in the Revolution.'

'Revolution?'

'Yes. Revolution. If that's what it takes.'

We go back to the town. It is full of people now and the salty air is a thick mix of hot dogs, onions, chips, and the burnt-sugar smell of candyfloss. No one is thinking about revolution, or anything much beyond having a good time. The rail is hot in my hands as I lean over it to look down at the beach filling with people setting out deckchairs and loungers, putting up windbreaks and umbrellas, laying claim to their part of the beach.

I buy her an ice cream. She asks for vanilla. She doesn't like other kinds. Only vanilla. We walk along the front. The booths are the same year on year: decorated with faded seaside scenes – fishing boats, a lighthouse, crabs, lobsters, starfish, a big octopus, bright colours rendered pastel by the winter and the salt in the air, peeling here and there, wood showing through. We walk on to the old pier and stop at the little funfair. She wants to go on the carousel. It's a period piece, with big, prancing horses on silver poles.

I get off. After a couple of rides the movement is making me feel a bit sick, but she gives the guy another tenner to go on riding the painted ponies round and round.

That's how I see her. The skirt of her dress blowing up to show her long, brown legs, her head back, her hair falling behind her, her eyes closed as she grips on to the barley sugar twist of the pole. The ancient-sounding fairground music jangles and wheezes as she turns and turns, locked in her own world.

25

Taking Jamie was far less of a hassle than going with his brother. Rob can be unpredictable and I didn't know how he would react but I had to see Theo and wanted Rob to meet him, too. We went to the funfair first, while I decided how I should handle it. He spent most of the time in the shooting arcades. I left him and went to ride the carousel. He won a load of stuff: teddy bears and fluffy toys that I took down to Oxfam. I had a few goes just to show him that I could. He said I've got what it takes. I'm guessing that was a compliment.

He was OK with sitting round the fire drinking beer and cider but I could tell that he didn't like Theo. Too much of an intellectual. Some of the others are anarcho-primitivists, Earth liberationists. It was pretty clear what Rob thought about them and he wasn't hiding it. The eco mob are supposed to be non-violent but I thought there

213

was going to be a fight. I was thinking it was all going pear-shaped and I should get him out of there, when this American showed up. This was the guy that Theo wanted Rob to meet. He'd deserted from the US Army, come here from Canada on a forged passport. He had fled what he saw as an illegal war. I didn't know how Rob would react to that.

They got talking and everyone else shut up. They are all anti-war – that's a given – but none of them has actually *been* in a war zone, seen the things that these two have seen. The American guy has their full attention as he recounts the events that led up to his desertion.

'I felt like every last drop of humanity was being squeezed out of me,' he says at last. 'Like I was turning into a killing machine. When they wanted to send me back for another term, I had to get out. I don't even blame the Taliban. I couldn't hate them any more, you know? Even when they were targeting our guys. All they're doing is defending their country. I blame the people who sent us there. They are the criminals in this.'

Rob nods, like he agrees, then he starts to tell them some of his own stories. He can be very eloquent when he wants to be, with an eye for little details that can turn your stomach or bring the tears pricking to your eyes. He can't seem to look away, and he makes sure that you don't, either. That's just how he is.

When their stories were exhausted, the beer finished, the fire dying back to ashy embers, the American just

*said goodnight and went off down the beach. I never
knew his name because he didn't say it and we didn't see
him again.*

*'It takes bollocks to do what that bloke did,' Rob said
afterwards. 'He's sound, but that Theo is a prick and the
rest of them are dicks. I don't want them involved with
this. And I don't know what you're doing with Jimbo, but
you can call time on that, too. He ain't got what it takes.
I don't want him anywhere near it. It's just me and you.'*

*He's right, of course. I'm thinking about that as I drive
Jamie back. I know Rob's right, but I just can't find the
words, the right way to do it.*

26

She drops me back home. Mum's out, the car is gone, but Martha's there. She hears my key and she's waiting for me. I dodge past her and make for the stairs. I need to shower and change.

'Alan called,' she yells after me. 'Wondering where you were.'

I stop halfway up the stairs. 'What did you tell him?'

'Said I had no idea.'

'Thanks, Martha. Thanks a lot. What did he say to that?'

'Said if you weren't there by this afternoon, you needn't bother turning up at all.'

'I better get down there. Square it with him.'

It's getting on for three o'clock. I run back down the stairs, my mind already reaching for excuses.

'You missed a good party,' she says as I make for the door. 'Lee was there.'

'I really don't have time for that right now.'

She ignores me and carries on with what she intended to say.

'She wanted to know if you'd finished with Caro yet.'

'None of hers. Or yours. Now, if you'll excuse me? Because of you I've got a job to save.'

'She said something else. That guy. The one she saw, coming out of Caro's? It wasn't you. Definitely. Know why?'

'No, Martha. I don't know why.'

I turn to face her. She has the look of a matador about to deliver the *estocada*.

'Because that guy walks with a limp.'

I grab my bike and take the side roads and back alleys. The quickest way to Rob's. When I get there, the curtains are drawn. I ring the bell but there is no reply. I hammer on the door. No response. Maybe he's out – or more likely back from the pub and sleeping it off. Either way, I'm here to have it out with him. If he's not in, I'll wait. Stuff Alan and his job. It's nearly the end of the summer, anyway. I'm not leaving until I get an answer.

I look around for the key that Grandpa used to keep under the brick, third geranium from the left. The plants have withered and died, crisp leaves on hollow brown twigs, but the key is still there.

I let myself in. The hall is quiet and dark. I shout out, but there is no reply. I'm coming back down the hall when

I sense rather than hear a movement upstairs. It's as though someone is up there, on the landing, hovering, waiting for me to go. I stop. There's definitely someone there.

'Rob?' I call. 'You there?'

Nothing. Just silence but the sense that someone is there is even stronger now. It doesn't have to be Rob. I feel the beginnings of fear creeping through my gut. Maybe it's a break-in. Someone up there and I've disturbed him. There's all kinds of stuff here. Not just Rob's stuff but Grandpa's medals. And his guns. I think about legging it out of there but I find myself gripping the banister and mounting the stairs.

'What the fuck are you doing here?'

Rob is standing at the top of the stairs in a pair of grey jersey trunks. The scarring livid on his leg. His arms folded, biceps bulging under his tattoos. He keeps in shape, doing weights, and it shows. His torso gleams with sweat like it's oiled, his stomach muscles ribbed and distinct beneath the powerful chest.

'I came over to ask you something. Then I thought there was someone upstairs . . .'

'Well there is. Me. As you can see. How did you get in?'

'I used the spare key from the garden. Grandpa used to keep one there.'

'Did he?' Rob frowns, like he knew that but had forgotten. His arms tighten across his chest. 'Well, I don't want every fucker in here all times of the night and day so you can just leave it on the table and go.'

'No. There's something I want to know.'

'Not now, Jimbo.'

He looks behind him. He's not alone. There's someone up there with him. That accounts for why he didn't answer, why he's upstairs in the middle of the day, why he's only wearing a pair of trunks, the sheen of sweat across his body.

'Yes. Now.'

I go to mount the stairs, determined to see who he's got up there. He comes down to meet me, barring my way.

'I said, not now!'

He takes me by one arm and turns me, forcing me back down the stairs. He frogmarches me to the front door, yanks it open, and suddenly I'm outside. The door slams and I hear the chain lock thrown across.

I step back and look up at the house, helpless. The curtains are open a bit now and he's standing at the window watching me. I can see a shape, an outline, the shadow of a girl. She comes up behind him and puts her arms around his waist. I can't see her face but silver flashes in the sun. She's wearing bracelets, lots of them. They slither down her arm as she reaches up to embrace him.

It could be another girl with bracelets, lots of girls wear bracelets, but I know it isn't. This is what's been in my head, but I didn't want to believe. A little, tiny bit of me was expecting a reprieve. It's like being in a car that is going to crash. Part of you is watching, *seeing* what is about to happen, but your brain can't accept, *won't* accept that this is it. I have that sick feeling deep inside me. This is *bad*. The kind of feeling you get when you lose something irreplaceable. You know that it has gone but still you look and look for it, revisiting the same places, not accepting that it is lost for ever.

I don't feel angry; I'm in a place beyond that. The betrayal is so deep, so complete, that I just feel empty, as though my insides have been hollowed out of me. I haven't felt like this since I was a kid when I'd run down the street crying because of something he'd done to me, some hurt or rejection, teased me beyond endurance. I don't cry now. I bite down hard on my lip until I taste blood in my mouth and just walk away, leaving my bike in the road, back wheel ticking. I don't look back. I know that nobody will be there.

27

Absinthe
n. 1. *A highly alcoholic bitter aniseed-flavoured spirit,*
usually green in colour, traditionally distilled from wine
*flavoured with wormwood (*Artemisia absinthium*) and other*
herbs, and served diluted with sugared water
Vanilla
n. *A pod produced by one or other species of the genus* Vanilla
Oxford English Dictionary

Absinthe and vanilla ice cream. Can't I like them both
at the same time? Aniseed, sharp at the root; vanilla,
sweet on the tip of the tongue. Can't I have a taste for
both of them?

Jamie is a nice boy but I'm a bitch to him. The nicer he
is, the more I want to hurt him. I can't seem to help it.
It's like cutting myself. It's a similar sensation, a similar
relief, although I'm watching someone else bleed. He
doesn't deserve to be with me. He deserves to be with
someone who's nice, like him, someone like Lee or Jesse
at the Rendez. *They both fancy him rotten but he can't*

see it. He's not vain, or conceited, or self-centred, like his friend Cal. He's good. A good person. Too good for me.

Rob is different. We deserve each other. We are perfectly matched.

Jamie would be better off with both of us out of his life. I'm glad he's found out about us. It's a relief. I was getting tired of the pretence. I couldn't think of a way of telling him without it causing a scene. Contrary to popular myth, I'm not a drama queen and I hate scenes – too many emotions on display and too many words spoken that should be left unsaid.

He was bound to find out sooner or later. I'm going to miss him but it's best that it happens now. Later could get complicated. The days are counting down.

28

I haven't seen her for more than a week now. I think about her every minute, rehearsing what I would do, what I would say. I haven't seen Rob, either. My bike appeared in the middle of the lawn. Other than that – nothing. Now that the numbness has receded, I want to kill him. The anger has solidified around me like lava flow.

Alan has taken me back and I work hard because it stops me thinking. I punt and row up and down all day like a wind-up toy and stay late to stack the deckchairs in the shed and secure the boats for the night. After that, it's straight down the pub with the lads from the boats. Every night, I get well and truly trashed; get into arguments, the occasional fight.

People are coming back from wherever they have been. I'm here waiting for them. It's all a bit mad. Everyone has been somewhere things were happening: Cornwall, festivals, Ibiza, travelling abroad, wherever. They want to be back there – or anywhere that isn't here. There are midnight picnics in the park, beach barbecues by the side of the municipal boating lake, cookouts on the common, house parties where people's parents are still away. Facebook and texts direct us to where it's happening. Awesome fun, Cal calls it, but it isn't really. Just endless excuses for piss-ups, ways of denying that term's coming on fast, the holiday's nearly over.

Cal and the other guys are in long shorts and flip-flops; Sophie and her friends stride about in pink wellingtons and teeny tiny shorts, or drift in floaty dresses desperate to carry on the summer, to do things before the tans fade, before the weather changes, finding ways to keep the illusion going that bit longer.

I've been nowhere. Done nothing except get my heart broken. I welcome them back, looking for diversion – anything to take my mind away from Caro. I'm free now. I can do what I want. 'You look different,' girls say, meaning more attractive all of a sudden. I'm deeply tanned from a whole summer on the river; I've got muscles from all that rowing and pushing the punts up and down. The OK-looking-but-nothing-special slightly shy but well-meaning kind of a guy goes without a goodbye. I don't care any more about anything very much and recklessness is attractive. The less interested I seem to be, the more girls fancy me. I'm doing OK, I tell myself. I'm having a good time. No. I'm having a *great* time. It's Saturday night and I'm at the sort of party I never got invited to before. I don't need Caro in my life, I'm thinking, while helping myself to a beer from a bin full of ice. All she's done is bring me trouble. I'm doing all right.

'Hi, Jamie.'

The voice is low and quiet. I think for one freezing second that it's her, but turn around to find Lee looking up at me.

'Oh, hi,' I say.

'No need to look so disappointed,' she says with an ironic half-smile.

'I'm not. Honest. Here.' I hold up the bottle. 'Do you want one of these?'

She nods, so I grab another beer. Everyone is outside in the garden of the house. It's noisy and crowded up on the patio, so I take her hand and guide her across the lawn to a bench between big rhododendron bushes. It's getting dark and I put my arm round her, ready to make a move, but she edges away.

'You're not with Caro any more?'

'Nah,' I take a drink, 'it's over. It didn't work out. Partly thanks to you. What you told Martha.'

'I'm sorry. I didn't mean for that to happen.'

I shrug, like no harm done, but she sees through it.

'I wasn't spying, or anything, and I didn't mean to cause trouble.'

'That's OK. I believe you. Martha did that for you.'

'I don't live far from her. I go for a run every morning. I saw someone leaving her place. I thought it was you. He *looked* like you, I even said hello, but it turned out –'

'Not to be me. Yeah. Seen him since?' I *hate* myself for asking.

'No,' she hesitates. 'I've seen you, though.'

Her voice is quiet, serious, with none of the brittle banter that's going on up on the terrace. She looks at me. Her dark eyes say she knows. She knows it's not over. Not over by a long way. For me, at least. What's the point in pretending? I have been out there, in the dead of night, in the early hours, watching until dawn and beyond, until the rattle of the one remaining milk round, the first commuters' cars starting in the drives, paper boys, post-man, recycling trucks. Sometimes stoned out of my mind, sometimes so pissed I could hardly walk, sometimes completely sober.

I haven't talked to anyone about her, about how I felt. Now I find myself pouring my heart out.

'She's not a bad person,' Lee says when I've finished. 'She's just not like anyone else. She plays by her own rules and she won't change. You have to decide to go along with it or leave the game.'

'Yes. I guess. I'm not sure I'm ready to do that yet.' That's the first time I've admitted that, even to myself. I look down. The bottle in my hands is empty. I get up to go and get another. 'Do you want one?'

'No.' She shakes her head. 'I think I'll be going.' She looks to the terrace where the laughter is getting louder, the behaviour more boisterous. 'Don't know why I came. I don't really like parties.'

I follow her gaze. Cal's having a mock fight with Suzy's new boyfriend. The girls are squealing as if they mean it. There's a chugathon going on round the beer bin, can cricket on the lawn.

'Yeah.' I laugh. 'I know what you mean. Hey, thanks for listening, though.'

'That's OK. I understand her better than most people. We were friends. Still would be if it was up to me. Still are in a weird kind of way. She cuts herself off, won't let anyone near her. It's not what people think. They say she's arrogant, that she thinks a lot of herself, that she's better than everyone else. It's the opposite of that. She's worried that if she let's anyone in, then they'll find out what's she's *really* like and run a mile. It's a deep-down hurt. You did well to get so close to her. She must really like you.' She reaches in her pocket for her phone. 'If you want to talk any time.'

We swap numbers and she goes. I don't stay that much longer. There is nothing for me here.

For once, I go home relatively sober and straight to bed. I go to sleep thinking of her, as always, but in the morning it is Rob who's in my mind. In the night, I'd woken up suddenly, like I'd been shaken, my body covered in sweat, the bedclothes twisted around me. I knew I'd been dreaming, but the dreams disperse quickly, like smoke in the wind, going beyond my conscious recollection. All I know, the only thing I can say for sure, is that Rob was in them all.

29

I go looking for him. This thing between us has to be settled one way or another. I cycle round to his place. No sign of him. I go to the pubs he uses and draw a blank there as well. I even buzz past *hers*. Her car isn't there, which I take as an indication that she's not, either. I don't want to see her, I'm not ready for that, so I don't go knocking on the door. The last place I try is the allotments. The plot is deserted.

I can't think where else to go. All that cycling has dissipated some of my energy. I decide to call it a day. The plum tree is laden and some of the apples look ready. While I'm here, I might as well do something useful, like pick some fruit for Grandpa. Mum can take it with her the next time she goes to the nursing home.

There should be plastic bags in the shed. I go to open the door and find it secured with a brand-new padlock. I look through the bleary little window. There are bags of stuff on the floor inside. Rob must have been down doing something. Looks like fertiliser, maybe he plans to dig the ground over and make it ready for next year, although Grandpa always preferred manure because it's more natural. There are some bottles with the skull and cross bones poison signs on the side. Must be weedkiller for the brambles.

I can put the fruit in my panniers. I start picking from the little orchard at the back of the plot. It's quiet here, peaceful, just the chatter from a couple of magpies and the distant sound of an engine being started, a mower, or a rotavator. I'm absorbed, selecting fruit. Not too soft – I don't want it squashing – not too green or it will be sour. I don't hear him until he's right behind me.

'What are you doing here?' he breathes in my ear.

Despite myself, I jump.

'Picking fruit. What does it look like?' I try to sound casual, but his sudden presence makes me shaky.

He steps back. He looks different. Sober and dressed all in black. I've never seen him wear black like that. Out of uniform, his taste runs from garish to ghastly. He's clean-shaven and his hair is cut short. He looks extra fit, like he's been working himself really hard.

'What have you been doing down here?' I ask, nodding towards the shed.

'Oh, this and that.'

'Why the new padlock?'

'Security. I'm storing some gear. I don't want it interfered with.'

'Break-ins?'

'Always the risk.'

I don't believe we're talking like this, with everything that has happened between us, that we're talking allotment business when all I really want to know is:

'Why are you screwing my girlfriend?'

He steps back, the sudden change of topic taking him by surprise. He looks at me, eyes shuttered.

'First off, she ain't your girlfriend, Jimbo. Mine, neither. Nobody owns a girl like that. Second –' He's grinning now, thumbs in his belt. 'Second, she offered. She's a great piece of ass, let's face it. Would have been rude to turn her down. Anyway, takes a man to handle that. I told you before.'

He turns with a shrug, as if that's it, as if my feelings in the matter count for about as much as the piece of fallen fruit he's toeing with the point of his boot.

'You can't just say that and walk away!'

'Can't I?' He doesn't even face me.

'It's always the same with you, Rob, isn't it?' I yell after him. 'Things get a little bit difficult and you bail. Maybe you don't want to know about the damage you do to people, or are you just too thick to see?'

He stops walking. I drop the pannier I'm holding, ready for his turning on me. All the anger, all the rage, I've been keeping in check, begins to flow. From some chamber deep inside, comes all the hurt, all the resentment I've ever felt, at every time I've been beaten, every time I've been bested. The two streams come together, seething and bubbling, rising and rising, ready to blow.

I take a run at him, bring him down in a crunching tackle. He's not expecting it. He's strong but I manage to hold him. Soon we're rolling around on the dusty ground and I'm getting some good punches into the ribs and kidneys but it's not enough. He turns me. I don't know how, but suddenly he's on top of me. He has his knee in my back and my neck in the crook of one arm. He tightens the lock until I'm fighting for breath.

He leans down, hissing the words close to my ear.

'I could kill you now. Break your neck. You know that?'

I struggle but it's futile. I can't shift his weight and every movement tightens his grip. It's like a steel hawser wrapped around my neck.

'Go ahead.' I choke the words out in a rasping cough. 'It's the only thing you know how to do. You psycho!'

'Don't call me that!'

The pressure increases until I nearly black out. He's pushing my face down so I taste the earth, feel the grit of it between my teeth. I can't breathe and I'm choking. Then he lets me go. I get up, spitting out a wad of mud. This is ending like every other fight we've ever had, with me beaten, eating dirt, and him walking away. He's almost at the end of the patch of ground. I take another run at him, launching into a two-footed flying tackle. I catch him on his bad side and he goes down, his face contorted in a howl. He rolls around, clutching at his leg and I'm on him. I'm sitting astride him, forcing him down. It's his turn to have his face in the dirt. The pain has sapped him, but he is struggling under me. He's so strong. I can't believe how strong he is. In a second he'll topple me and our roles will be reversed. What will he do to me then? I reach out, groping around until my hand closes round the sharp angles of a half-brick. I pick it up, holding it rough edge pointing down, ready to smash it into the back of his head.

'Enough!' A woman's voice shouting. 'That's enough!' I look up and she's standing on the path, watering can poised, ready to empty the contents over us. 'It works with cats. Dogs too. Why not young men? Get up the both of you.'

I roll off him and scramble to my feet. Rob's having trouble standing but I don't help him. The woman offers her hand instead. I recognise her. It's Brenda from the next allotment.

'You're Fred's grandsons, aren't you? I remember you scrapping like that when you were lads but you're a bit big for it now. Pity you don't use some of that energy getting the place tidy for your grandfather. Now shake hands.'

We stare at each other, reluctant, but she's not going to budge until we do. He puts his hand out. I take it.

'Properly now.'

I grip harder.

'That's better.' She nods, satisfied, and she goes on her way.

Her intervention has dispelled the anger between us. I don't want to fight any more. Neither does he.

'You had me there.' He nods towards the brick. 'Thought I was a goner.'

'I wouldn't have done it. Not really.'

'Maybe not, but you need to finish what you start. That's what they teach you in the Army. You got balls, though. More than I took you for.' He points a finger like a gun at my head. 'Respect.'

We sit on the rickety little bench in front of the shed and he lights a cigarette.

'I wasn't that bad to you, was I? When we were kids?'

'Yeah. You were.'

'Not all the time, surely? I used to give you stuff. Tell you stories. I got you that Genesis bike you're riding.'

'It was knock-off! The stuff you used to give me was bust half the time and the stories you told me were lies.'

'There is that.' He laughs, like it's a joke that we can share now. 'Sometimes it's better than knowing the truth.'

'Is it? I'm not sure about that.'

'Believe me, there's things you are better off not knowing.'

'Like about Dad? About him killing himself?'

'How do you know about that?'

'Caro told me.'

'She shouldn't have done that.'

'Maybe not, but I'm glad she did. Have you always known? Is that what the stories were about?'

'No. The stories were about something different. I only found out about the old man recently. Grandpa told me when he'd had too many Johnnie Walkers. Ma doesn't know I know. She should have told us, though.'

Yeah, she should, but I can kind of understand it. Tell a lie long enough and you begin to believe it. We all have to find our own way to keep our sanity.

'Maybe she was saving us from feeling any kind of stigma.' I automatically seek to make excuses for her. 'Especially because he was a soldier. Shouldn't be, but for some people there's still a certain amount of shame attached.'

'Shouldn't be. You're right there. But with so many guns about, it's more common than you'd think.'

'Did you – I mean, did you ever –'

'Not when I was in. Never crossed my mind then, but I know it happens.'

'Now?'

He doesn't answer straight away.

'Perhaps. Maybe I'm cursed that way. Like the old man. Some things you can't break, you know? Like I was mean to you, even when I didn't want to be. I couldn't seem to help myself. The old man was the same way with me. Maybe it's in our genes.'

'No!' I don't like him talking like this. 'That's bullshit, Rob! Genes don't work like that. And, anyway, if they did, if you've got them, then I've got them. Martha, too.'

'You two take after Mum.' He looks down at the

cigarette. 'She don't smoke, neither do you. The old man did, though. Could run that way with me. Through the father, like. People don't kill themselves for nothing.'

His reasoning is all over the place. It doesn't make sense, but if it's what he believes, it will be hard to talk him out of it. He's stubborn like that.

'Is that how you feel?' I have to ask him straight out. 'That you want to kill yourself?'

'I don't know. Sometimes. Maybe. Or . . .' He shakes his head and puts his hand up to his temple, as though the action hurt him. 'I'm telling you, Jimbo. The drugs don't work no more. Booze, neither. I've gotta find some way to ease it.' It's as though he's talking about a physical pain, something that can be alleviated. 'All this shit inside me. It's building. Like how you feel before a battle, or a firefight, but there's no way for it to come out . . .'

'Perhaps you need to go back to therapy.'

'Bollocks to that! I've had that. It doesn't work.'

'Maybe they didn't find the *right* treatment.'

He looks at me with weary disappointment, like he expected me to understand something and I've failed.

'Fuck that. There is no *right* treatment because there *is* no treatment. I'm beyond treatment.' He takes one last drag and flips his fag away. 'Gotta man up. Do what's needed.' He gets up from the bench and tests his leg, wincing as he puts his weight on it. 'Whoa! You really hurt me, you know?'

238

I'd almost forgotten about the fight, although my neck is sore and my arm hurts from where he twisted it.

'Sorry,' I say.

'Me, too.' He laughs. 'Ain't sure she's really worth fighting over.'

'Caro?'

'Who else?'

'I've finished with her, anyway. It's over.'

'How do you know she's finished with you?' He gives me a crooked grin. 'Be careful of her. She's a dangerous girl. Take care of yourself, little bro.'

30

Good thing I got a new lock for the shed. Jimbo's a nosy little bugger. I've been busy since that little trip to the seaside. Making preparations, getting ready – you're only as good as your planning.

While I work I get to think about things – like how that Yank was right. People being blown up there every day – their side, our side. Innocents caught in the middle. Every day someone somewhere gets the knock. *His family have been informed* – but who the fuck else cares. They've moved on to the next news item – like those bastards bricking Dixons and nicking stuff from PC World. No one cares about that poor fucker brought back in a box.

They have to be made to care – nothing like a bit of death and carnage for getting the message across.

Caro likes to think I've bought into all that political crap she spouts on about but I'd do it anyway because she asked me – because it needs doing, because it's what I do – what I'm good at. I look at it like a job. I don't think about all that political shit – I just know it's the right thing and since I committed to this and started to get into the preparation I've been happier than I've been for a long long time.

Her and her friends think they're smart but I know stuff they don't – like what kind of materials to use and how to handle them and what kind of gun you need for what job. You don't need an M107 – although it would be nice to have one. All you need is a high-powered hunting rifle with a decent sight. I got one of those courtesy of her stepfella – old Trevor. A Weatherby Mark V Accumark 30-378. I don't know what old Trev was planning on hunting but that gun is one of the best there is. Accurate up to 500 metres, so they say. So you need that and you need a good vantage point. Checked a few out before going for the multi-storey. It's the perfect spot – awaiting demolition so the place is boarded up. There's CCTV but it's all pointing in the wrong direction – easy to dodge. The stairs are blocked off so I go up the ramps. I check the spot every other day to look for any sign of work starting, dossers – skateboarder activity – wouldn't want any surprises. It takes me longer than usual to get to the top with my leg thanks to Jimbo but when I get up there I know why I picked it – hell of a good position. I've got a hide up there made out of plastic sheeting coated with cement dust and bits of rubble – if there were to be a search they would never find me – they'd expect me to be out in the open like some tool – I crawl under the plastic pulling the edge over me like a hood. I take my scope with me – an S&B 5-25x56 day scope – plus state-of-the-art telescopic day and night all-weather sights x3-x12 x 50. Sight and spotting scope courtesy of the British Army.

I lie up with the whole town spread out on four sides of me – I could stay here for hours.

There will be security – no doubt – but he's not exactly the President of the United States. They won't be patrolling every high-rise in the town – they'd judge this out of range in any case. Plenty better spots a lot nearer than this – not many would be able to make the hit from here.

Not many. Except me.

31

It's the bank holiday. One of our busiest times. The weather has just been getting hotter. Everyone says there has to be a storm soon, that it can't last. It's all as per normal down by the river: kids playing, babies crying, people picnicking. There's the smell of onions from the hotdog stand. I'm wondering whether to go over and get one, and for once I'm not thinking about her, when, suddenly, there she is. All sounds, all other senses recede, as I watch her walk down from the bridge, bag slung over her shoulder. Her skin is brown, as though she has spent the intervening time sunbathing. She's wearing dark glasses against the sun's glare and a short dress with thin straps and bright red flowers all over it, made of some silky material that ripples in the breeze coming up from the river. She looks wonderful, mysterious and glamorous but I'm not ready to forgive her, even when she walks up and kisses me on the cheek, just like we are the couple I wanted us to be. She puts her hand on my arm and whispers, 'Are you for hire?'

'No,' I say, trying to keep myself steady. The boat is rocking, water slapping against the side of the dock. 'If you really want to go on the river, you'll have to take one of the other boats.'

I load up and push off.

When I get back, she's still there, waiting. Sitting on a bench, eating an ice cream. Vanilla. It's her favourite. She doesn't like other kinds. She always has vanilla.

She comes down to the station to meet me.

'I'm next in line and I've paid my money.' She steps into the punt. 'What are you going to do? Throw me out?'

I want to. I think about it. That's what I *should* do. But I don't. We do need to talk and it would be better to go somewhere quiet. It's way too crowded here. I push away from the bank towards the middle of the river.

'What do you want, Caro? What are you doing here? Why don't you leave me alone?'

'Because I want to talk to you. I don't want us to finish that way.'

'What *us* are you talking about, exactly? I didn't think there was an *us* – you've made that clear enough. You can't have everything you want, just because you want it, Caro. When are you going to learn that?'

'The thing with Rob. It's not what you think.'

'Isn't it? Seems clear to me.'

'That thing at his house? Just a booty call.'

'And I'm supposed to put up with that? You going to see him whenever you fancy it? He's my *brother*.'

'It means nothing.'

'To you, maybe.'

'It's different with you. More . . .' She pauses, trying to find the right word. 'Meaningful.'

'Oh, really?' This is all bullshit and I'm not having any. 'You could have fooled me.'

'I never wanted to hurt you, Jamie.'

'Well, you did. You have. If you'd thought for a month, you couldn't have done a better job. I really loved you, y'know? And you did that to me.'

'I don't do love.'

'You've made that crystal.'

I narrowly miss a dinghy. I'm poling so hard, the punt is moving through the water like it's turbo-charged.

'Let's go to the ait.' Water is slopping into the shallow craft, splashing her arms. 'You'll have us both in the river at this rate.'

'Not a bad idea.' I plunge the pole in with a vicious thrust. 'Perhaps I'll take us straight over the weir.'

But, of course, I don't. I land at our usual place.

I moor the boat and follow her through the curtain of willows towards the further island. Her step across the weir is as light as ever, firm and sure. I follow. I hop over the displaced stone, too angry to feel any fear. The river water pools behind it, clear and deep. I remember when we swam there. It's full of God knows what crap. I must have been mad.

'What do you want?'

'I want you back.'

She pulls me to her and we don't do much talking after that. I hate myself, *hate* myself, but she's so close and so near and I can't resist her. It's over almost before it has begun. She has her eyes closed, her face turned away from me. It's always been the same way with her. I realise that now. At the moment when you're supposed to feel the ultimate togetherness, I end up feeling most alone.

She wants me back, does she? Things are never how you want them to be. I strip off the condom and throw it into the bushes to join the others. Just like the river water – the ait looks clean but it isn't. It's full of all kinds of trash: empty cans, faded plastic bags, bleached and wrinkled scraps of paper. It's not exactly a paradise. It's a hot day, but suddenly I've got gooseflesh creeping over me. I pull on my clothes.

'Summer's nearly over,' she says. 'It always makes me sad.'

The poplars have that tired, dull green look, the leaves crisping at the edges, and the willows are already turning brown and yellow. The shops in town are full of back-to-school displays. Pencil cases to be replenished, calculators and memory sticks purchased, along with trousers and shirts that no one would be seen dead in and cheap polyester blazers that some poor sods still have to wear. In

July, it always seems like the summer will go on for ever. There's always going to be plenty of time.

'What are you thinking?' she asks.

'I was thinking you're right. Summer's nearly over.' I get to my feet and help her up. 'We'd better be getting back.'

Out on the river, the water is the colour of gunmetal. The atmosphere is heavy and humid. The clouds banked above the town are slaty purple. The storm is near.

'Have to hurry if we're not going to get a soaking.'

Just as I say it, there is a lurid scribble of lightning and the crack of thunder, like a branch breaking. Big drops of rain splash down on the wood of the punt and dimple the water. I pole us back down the river as fast as I can. The other boats are in and Alan is beckoning. A thunderstorm is not a good time to be out on the river.

I help her out. The others are all huddled in the hut, but I don't invite her to shelter there. She has no coat, or umbrella, but she doesn't dash for cover – she walks away slowly, her dress clinging to her. Her flimsy, high-heeled sandals wobble on the slippery cobbles. She looks lonely, vulnerable in the rain-swept world. I want to run after her, give her shelter, but I don't do that. I just watch as she rights herself and continues on her way, up the steps to the bridge.

32

H minus 25.30

Recon.

I get into position early and scope out the kill box. There's something going on – car park filling. I check my watch. 8.31 – some kind of pre-term meeting.

As they get out of their cars I mark 'em – one by one.

Pinky – Mr Perkins – dragging his sorry arse out of his shit Ford Focus. Still there then. I remember him – Careers. Fat lot of use he was. When I told him I was going to join the Army – he said 'You deserve each other' and laughed in a sarky way – eyes sliding to the rest of the class like he expected them to join in but they never did because they didn't like him and were shit scared of me. Lost more hair I see but still wearing what he has left long and swept back – yes – give it a pat – and his nose stuck up like he's got a smell under it. Those glasses flashing in the sun make a good target – I'd slot him through the right eye or maybe bisect the gold rims. I feel the twitch in my trigger finger, the itch to do it.

Suit No Tie Job – must be the Head or Principal. He's arriving in a BMW and the rest of 'em all drive skips. He's got his jacket slung over his shoulder – I'd get him through the phone in his top pocket – right in the apps.

Barney – Barney Rubble. We used to call him that because he looked like that character in *The Flintstones*. He's running over to Suit No Tie – always was a brown-nose. Where's the trackie Barney? He's suited and booted like the head guy – must have been promoted. Still dyeing his hair. That little bald spot at the back – that's a bull's eye.

The little blonde one – English teacher – she was all right – pass on her.

That one too – PE bird. Used to fancy her – pass on her an' all.

Not him though – bastard French teacher – knobhead. He used to say I was thick – used to take the piss. Definitely not passing on him – he's slotted.

I'd forgotten how much I hated them.

Seems a waste not to take them down while I'm at it – all the little ducks coming across to be slotted – like the shooting arcade.

It's a while since I had this much fun.

www.urflixstar.com/robvid

33
PROPAGANDE PAR LE FAIT –
PROPAGANDA OF THE DEED

They are 'delayed' in France, according to an email sent on my mother's Blackberry at 9.35. Trouble with the ferries. First I've heard of it. I checked the Internet. She just wants another week in France. It will all be over by then. One way or another.

Jamie is an innocent, the tarot card Fool. I want him to stay that way. I do not want him to be involved. He wouldn't go along with it, anyway. He lacks commitment to any kind of belief system, as far as I can see, and is likely to be overwhelmed by emotions that don't bother his brother, like empathy and pity. He also has a conscience, another thing that doesn't trouble Rob.

I don't want to involve him but I want to say goodbye to him. I feel like I owe him something and after tomorrow, we won't be seeing each other. Ulrike, Gudrun, Astride, Petra, the women in the Red Army Faction, look down on me from the wall. What did they feel before they went on actions? Did they suffer from nerves? Did time go too slow for them or too fast? Did they wonder if they could do it, really, when it came right down to it? Wonder if they were capable of killing people?

They proved they could do it, but they are all dead now. I have to face that possibility, too.

The gap between theory and practice is wide. It yawns wider as the hours crawl by. I feel as though I'm right on the edge and the ground is crumbling, falling away from beneath my feet. I'm committed to this action but bourgeois feeling could still get the better of me, or my own courage could fail me, or –

I need a distraction. I'm going to call Jamie. I need to see him. I'm going to miss him, bizarre as that seems, even to me. I'd go and get him right now – we could go off somewhere, if I stay here I could go crazy – but Rob's got my car. Doesn't trust the brake pads and it's all got to be right for the morning. No cock-ups. So Jamie better come here. I'll get things in, have them delivered. Make it special.

If I didn't know myself better, I'd be wondering if I might be entertaining bourgeois feelings for him, but I don't do love. I told him that. I've been cruel to him, treated him in ways he doesn't deserve. This will be my last chance to make it up to him.

He'll have to be gone by the morning. He mustn't be here when Rob comes around.

34

College starts tomorrow. I've done nothing all summer. Across the landing, Martha is dragging bin bags about, having a clear out, getting ready for uni. Cambridge. She's got her place. She's already been down to the library with her reading list, even though term doesn't start for weeks yet. Everything she does is some kind of reproach, designed to show me up. My files and folders are still on the shelf above my desk. Untouched. I get up and go over to the haphazard pile that has been there since I dumped the contents of my rucksack. My finger draws a line through the pale, fine dust of summer made up of all sorts of stuff, pollen from flowers now dead and withered, sand blown all the way from the Sahara, particles of my own skin.

I think about getting ready. Rather than actually doing anything, I log on to the school website, see if there is anything I need to know. Just opening it makes me feel queasy. There's a cheesy PR photo of the Principal, his Message to the Masses and a promo for the Grand Opening. I can't get into the Student Area. They've been dicking about with the site again. Good excuse for not doing anything. I'll have a bit of time to catch up. That does something to quell the sick feeling. Then my phone goes and my stomach flips again. A message from Caro.

She wants to see me.

Mine 2nite 7:30 dress smart

I don't reply straight away. I leave the phone on the desk and go lie on the bed. I don't want her thinking she's out and free. I'm still not OK with what she did to me. I get up and go downstairs to make a cup of coffee. I don't want her thinking that she's got me where she wants me, or that I'm back to being the same old loser. I leave it a definite while before I text her. Then I'm tearing clothes out of the closet, trying this, trying that. I opt for the Jack Wills chinos I've just bought and the shirt she gave me, all neatly washed and pressed. I put a jacket in my rucksack with a change of clothes for tomorrow. Just on the off chance she'll let me stay. The idea of arriving in her car does have a certain appeal.

I'm not really concentrating – taking quick ways, cutting corners, and I almost run right into Lee. She's coming out of a side road. She's wearing shorts, vest and running shoes, like she's into proper training. She has a dog on one of those extendable leads that look like clothes lines. I nearly total the mutt.

'I didn't see you. I'm really sorry.' I get off my bike to see that they are all right. 'Hey, fella.' I lean down to pet the little dog. He snarls a bit and snaps at me. I take that for a 'yes'.

'It's a girl,' she says. 'Mitzy.' She kneels down to check her over. 'She's a cairn terrier. She's fine.' She straightens up again. 'You should look where you're going. Shouldn't be riding on the pavement, anyway.'

'Yeah, I know.'

'Where are you off to in such a hurry?' She pretends to think. 'Let me guess.'

'That obvious?'

She smiles. 'That obvious. You two back together again?'

'Maybe. I hope so.'

'If that's what you want.'

'It is at the moment.'

'If you ever get her out of your system, I'll be around.' She tugs the lead. 'Come on, Mitzy. Let's go.'

She sets off, the mutt running along beside her. The dog's a fast mover for such a small breed.

Caro opens the door and puts her arms round me. She seems glad to see me.

'Thanks for coming over,' she says after a while.

'Folks still not back?'

She shakes her head. 'Delayed at Calais. I didn't want to be alone. Not tonight.'

I laugh. 'It's only school starting. And it's not as though you don't know anyone.' I put my arms round her again. 'Me for a start.' I push a lock of hair back behind her ear. 'I'll be there to take care of you. I'll see that you're all right.'

She smiles up at me. 'I know you will.' She holds me away from her. 'Not bad. You scrub up well. Come on.' She hangs my bag up in the lobby and takes me by the hand, leading me into the living room. 'I've got a surprise. Wait here. Help yourself to a drink.'

She leaves me there and disappears upstairs. She's away quite a while.

There's music playing, jazz or something, on low. There's a bucket with champagne chilling and a bottle of vodka. I go into the kitchen and fetch myself a beer.

It's worth the wait. When she comes downstairs, she looks like a girl from a dream. Like no one else I've seen, as if she's not quite real but has stepped out of the screen. Her hair falls in a deep wave across her face and her eyes look huge under fine, arched brows, her cheekbones shadowed, her lips are painted deep red. The dress she's wearing is low-cut and clings to her, shimmering as she moves.

'You look amazing,' I say.

She smiles and comes towards me. She's wearing high heels, so she's nearly as tall as me. There's a looking glass on the wall above the mantelpiece. She puts her arm through mine and we stand together. For a second we seem like two strangers in the mirror, neither quite knowing what to say next or what to do. I feel like I'm looking at a vision of the future, not as we are now, but as we might be one day. I know at that moment that I want to spend the rest of my life with her. One day, I will ask her to marry me. Neither of us says anything, but there is a gleam at the corner of her eye, like glycerine. She doesn't have to say it, I know that she feels the same way I do.

'I want tonight to be special,' she says.

She's ordered weird food off the Internet, caviar and foie gras, quail eggs. She likes that kind of fancy stuff, but the eggs are too hard to peel, and I don't like the fishy taste of the caviar or the way the globules pop in my mouth. The paté is too rich and I remember Martha telling me how they stuff the geese with grain to get it. In the end, we order a takeaway. We drink the champagne with chicken tikka jalfrezi and rogan josh.

After we've eaten, she brings in a bottle of Oaxaca mescal, the one with a scorpion floating in the bottom of the bottle, and a dish piled with segments of lime and two salt-rimmed glasses. I remember the last time and opt for vodka.

She pours two shots. 'Here's to us.'

She downs the vodka and throws the glass into the fire-place. I follow suit. We do it again and fall about laughing.

We play drinking games and generally mess around. We don't talk about Rob. We don't talk about the past and we don't try to look into the future. We stay strictly in the present. It's the best time I've ever had with her. All that matters is here and now.

I'm just thinking that, when she gets up to check her phone. I didn't hear it; maybe she's had it on silent. She checks the text messages and her face changes.

'You'll have to go.'

'What time is it?' I grope around for my watch. I lost it in some kind of forfeit.

'12.30.'

'Do I have to?' I roll over and look up at her. 'I thought I could stay. We could go in together.'

I'm genuinely disappointed. To stay the whole night has become a bit of a mission. Now we are back together, I've got things I want to say to her.

'So did I.' She shows every sign of feeling the same way but she always was a good actor. 'But it's just not possi-ble.' She shakes her head and begins collecting my clothes. 'I've just had a text. They got a late ferry. They'll be back before morning.'

'OK. OK.' I'm hopping round, trying to get my leg down my trousers. That's different. I don't want to be caught by her mother and an irate stepdad.

'See you tomorrow.'

'Yeah. See you tomorrow.'

She gives me a last kiss, her lips gliding over mine, smooth and dry like silk. When she looks up at me there are tears in her eyes.

35

I don't know what wakes me. My head is hammering and my mouth feels like the bottom of a badger sett. I roll over and check the clock. 7.00. Way too early. I go to roll back, to sleep again for another hour at least, when I hear it again. The sound that woke me. A message coming into my phone.

I'm out of bed in a second and groping in my chinos' pocket. It's not from her. I sit back down on the end of the bed again, disappointed, thinking about the time I could have had, if only her folks had not been coming back. If only she had let me stay. It's from Lee. What can she want?

I open the message.

Just seen ur bro @ C's house

I stare at it stupidly. I want to think there is a simple explanation, but can't help assuming the obvious. She's messing me around yet again. My stomach gets that hollowed-out feeling as I put down the phone and start dragging on my clothes.

I jump on my bike. It's early. There's not much traffic about. I'm over there in record time. I punch in the combination and the gate swings open, closing behind me as I slip inside. I take a wary look at the upstairs windows but the blinds are shut. I skirt round her car parked in the drive. It wasn't there last night, which is odd. No sign of her folks' SUV. I go to the side gate. It has the same combination as the main gate. I enter the numbers, meaning to go round the back, see what I can spot through the windows. There's no one downstairs. The big room is empty, so is the kitchen. I move round towards the conservatory. She sometimes forgets to lock it. The amount she had to drink last night that is a distinct possibility, although she has tidied up. The kitchen window shows bottles stacked next to the recycling bins and there's no sign of the takeaway trays. The surfaces are clean. That's not like her. When I left last night, the kitchen looked like a kebab shop on a busy night. Unless she doesn't want Rob to know she's been entertaining. But that is the only indication that he might be here. Maybe Lee was wrong about that and I'm wasting my time.

Only one way to find out. I try the conservatory door, gently, slowly easing the handle. It's one of those you have to push up and pull out a little bit. I hear the rods release. It is open.

I glide in, careful not to make any noise. The door

makes the faintest click as I close it behind me. No tell-tale creaking. UPVC does have some advantages. The door into the living room opens without a sound. No indication of last night's carnage. Everything neat and tidy in here, too. I check out the lobby. No sign of the returning family – that was just a lie to get rid of me – but my ruck-sack is there, hanging from the coat rack. I'd forgotten all about that. I move towards the foot of the stairs with more confidence. I'm not a burglar or a deranged stalker; I have an excuse to be here.

I'm just about to go up and confront them, when I hear noises. First Caro, then Rob. So he *is* here. I can't hear what they're saying. They are talking low, as if someone might overhear them. Considering there's no one else here, that strikes me as strange. I get to the top of the stairs. Her bedroom is empty. The voices are coming from the little room at the end of the landing. Trevor's study.

'Are you ready?' I hear him say.

'Yes, I'm ready.'

I go back down the stairs to wait. Maximum surprise.

Rob comes down first. He's carrying a holdall in one hand. A long gun case in the other. I feel an impulse to run and hide, but I stand my ground.

He stops, genuinely rocked back. His grip on the gun case tightens.

'What are you doing here?'

'Could ask the same.'

'It's not what you are thinking.'

'Oh, and what am I thinking?' I can't take my eyes off the gun case. I don't know what to think.

'It's best if you go,' he says. 'Go now.'

'Yes.' Caro says from the stairs. 'Go now. It will be better if you do.'

I look up to where she's coming down behind him. She's wearing a combat jacket with the red star badge on it. Baader-Meinhof. The Red Army Faction. I've done my research. Urban guerrillas. Direct Action. Active in Germany in the 1970s. Killed I don't know how many people. But it's just an entry on Wikipedia, right? No one would be mad enough to pull stunts like that now.

I look from one to the other. They are both wired. Whatever is going down here is deadly serious. It was all there for me to see, except I've been walking round like a man in a dream, looking at things, with no idea of their meaning or what they might signify.

I remember the school website. *Forthcoming Events at Egmont Academy.* The Grand Opening. The VIP, a distinguished politician, honouring our school by coming to cut the ribbon.

I should run while I still can, while they are both on the stairs. Get out of there, call the police, alert the authorities, but I don't do any of that. Rob's got guns. He won't go quietly. There'd be a stand-off. A siege with armed police. SWAT teams. He'll use her as a hostage. She could be killed, either way. I have to try and stop it right here. Now.

'I'm not going anywhere.'

'Yeah, you are.' Rob looks down at me. 'You're going to school, like a good little boy.'

Funny thing is, I think Caro might say something now, like *Don't go to school*, even at the risk of giving it away, just to save me, but she doesn't. I get a cold feeling, like my insides are congealing. She cares more about this, about whatever they are planning, than she does about me.

'I know what you are going to do.'

'Oh, yeah?' Rob snarls. 'What's that?'

They look at each other, then back at me.

'I don't know for sure, but I think you're going to –' I pause, trying to stop my voice from shaking at the enormity of what they are intending, at the strain of confronting them, putting it into words. 'I think that you're planning an attack on the school.'

It sounds mad as it comes out of my mouth.

'How do you know that?' Rob's voice is quiet, almost casual, but the words come out slow and ominous. He looks up at Caro. 'You told him, didn't you?' He shakes his head slowly, like she's disappointed him. 'You stupid bitch.'

'No, she didn't tell me. I got a text from a friend saying you were here. I guessed the rest.' I nod towards the gun he's carrying. 'Doesn't take a genius.'

He comes down the stairs towards me and I'm glad the gun is still in the case. His face is white and tight and he has that blank look in his eyes. I take a step away from him. I'm trying to be cool, but he's scaring me.

'You can't do this,' I say, trying to keep my voice low, stop it squeaking up into panic falsetto.

'I think you'll find we can.'

'Let him go, Rob,' Caro says from her place on the stairs. 'He's not part of this.'

'No.' He shakes his head. 'No can do. He's made himself part of it. Good thing I came equipped.' He holds the bag up. 'I got all I need to secure him. Duct tape, plastic ties for wrists and ankles.' He looks around. 'We'll have to stow him here.'

Caro shakes her head. 'I just had a text from my mother. They got the night ferry. They could be back any time.'

'Christ! I thought you said they were away for the week?'

'Change of plan.'

'For fuck's sake! He'll have to come with us, then. With me.' He turns to her. 'I'll leave him up the multi-storey. Someone will find him eventually. No one jeopardises this operation. Not him. Not you. No one. You get me?' He pushes me in front of him. 'OK. Let's roll.'

We go out into the bright autumn morning. I see Caro shiver, either at the coldness of the air, or maybe the reality of what they plan to do is coming home to her. She touches the remote control that she keeps on her car keys and the gates glide open on a world that couldn't be more normal. Men dressed in shirtsleeves are slinging briefcases and computer bags into the backs of their cars, hanging up their suit jackets. Mums are coming out to do the school run, packing kids into the back of people carriers, passing them bright new bags and shiny new lunchboxes, ready for the new school year.

This is my last chance to stop this thing from happening. I refuse to get in the car.

'Get in!' He takes out a handgun from his pocket. His eyes flick to the happy families. 'Or it starts right here.'

I get in the car. He gets in the other side, moves over so he's sitting behind me. I feel the end of the gun barrel, small and round and cold on the back of my neck.

Caro tries to start the engine, the ignition squealing. She fumbles the gears.

'Don't go flaky on me,' he says. 'Time's wasting.'

She finally gets the car started and drives out on to the road.

'Drive carefully now,' he says to her. 'Don't do anything to draw attention and mind the speed bumps.'

He jabs the gun into the back of my neck again. A reminder not to act up and not to turn round.

'Why would you even think about doing this?'

'Direct action,' Caro supplies. 'It is the only way to get people to pay attention. Propaganda of the deed.'

'See how they like it,' Rob says behind me. 'Right, Caro?'

'Violence is the only way to answer violence,' Caro says, although she's not sounding too sure, now it's really going to happen.

'That's bullshit and you know it!' I turn to look at her, even though he jabs the gun barrel in harder. 'How's this going to make a difference?'

She doesn't answer. Her grip on the wheel tightens. Anxiety makes her speed up and we bounce over one traffic calming device then another.

'Slow down! I told you to watch that!' Rob shouts from the back, his voice loud with something I've never heard there before. Something like fear. 'Keep your speed down! There's a load of explosives packed into the spare wheel!'

'What?' Caro turns her head to face him and the car swerves, hitting the kerb.

'Fuck's sake! I said – drive careful!'

'You never said anything about a bomb!'

'You wanted an operation. You got one. *Violence is the only way to answer violence.*' He is parroting her words back at her.

'A bomb? For Christ's sake, Rob.' I twist, trying to see him. 'That's crazy! The whole thing's crazy! You've got to stop this right now.'

'Don't say that.' He angles the gun up under my skull. 'I've told you before.'

'But why would you do that? Caro?' I turn to appeal to her. 'This is madness. You can't do this. Think of all the people who'll be there! All the people who could get killed!'

'You shut up! You ain't got no say in this. No say at all. I told you, didn't I? Should have done me when you could.'

'A bomb isn't part of it. Was never part of it.' Caro is

trying to keep calm, but her hands are trembling, slipping on the wheel. 'This was supposed to be a political operation, an assassination.'

'Dead is dead. You said that yourself. What does it matter who or how many? See how they like it here, that's what you said. *Direct Action. It is the only way to get people to pay attention.*' He's quoting her words back at her again, taunting her with her own rhetoric. 'You thought I weren't listening, couldn't understand all that political stuff you were laying on me. I was listening all right. I ain't thick.'

'I never said you were.' She says it so quietly he can't hear.

'What's that?'

'I never said you were thick.'

'Yeah? It's what you think, though? Him, too. I'm just doing what you said you wanted. Do anything for you, wouldn't I, princess? A bomb on home soil, in a school? That should do it. That'll make a difference. That'll get their attention. It certainly will.'

Caro has no reply. Rob can't see her face but I can. It is pale, like a mask, no expression, but her lips are trembling, tears beginning to slide down her cheeks.

'You listen up,' he says to her. 'You listen to me and you listen carefully. This is what you are going to do. You will drop me and Jimbo at the multi-storey, then you will drive to the school. You will park your car on the side of the car park which is parallel to the drive.'

'When is it set to go off?' Her voice is far away, almost disinterested, as if she's distancing herself from the whole thing.

'10.15. I open up at 10.00. It's a trick they use all the time out there. Double whammy. One thing goes down and everyone thinks that's it. Just when they think it's all over – kerboom! If one don't get you, the other one will.' He gives a low laugh, as if at something private, not meant to be funny. 'I'll be watching so no-show from you, car in the wrong place, anything don't look right, and I start shooting, beginning with Jimbo. Any sign of trouble, things not going according to plan, he gets it first.'

'And what if there are car checks? What if they stop me? Search the car?' There's that distance again, as if she's talking about someone else who's been given the task of driving a car bomb into a school.

'That's your problem, darlin'. You'll think of some-thing. Sweet talk them. Use your charm. Or schwack!'

He's holding the gun up to my head now. She glances sideways and back again. Rob has taken this way past anything that she had planned. He's hijacked the whole mad scheme and then outmanoeuvred her with all the skill of a grand master. She's silent, like she has no answers. He's left her with nowhere to go.

Her tears have dried on her face. Her jaw is rigid; a small muscle jumps in her cheek. She's driving smoothly now, with more confidence, but her knuckles are white where she's gripping the wheel. Her apparent indifference is masking her anger. She is fighting to keep her fury under control.

'Rob!' I twist round. We are nearing the town now, minutes away from the multi-storey car park. Up there, he'll have the whole town in front of him, not just the school. Precinct, ring road, you name it. I know he's beyond reasoning, but I have to try. I figure he won't shoot me, not here, not now, not in a street full of cars and people. 'You can't –'

I don't get to finish the sentence.

'I told you to shut the fuck up!'

He hits me across the side of the head hard with the barrel of the gun. I see double, can't hear for the ringing in my ears and feel the liquid trickle beginning to flow through my hair. I touch my forehead. My hands come away red with blood.

Caro turns to look at me, automatically lifting her foot from the accelerator as she does so.

'Don't stop the car,' he snarls at her. We're driving through the centre of town, towards the bridge over the river. There are plenty of people about, getting off buses, walking up from the station, coming out of cafes clutching lattes. 'Keep driving or he gets it – you, too, and anyone else around.'

For a second, I think that she is going to disobey him. Her eyes go wide with shock at the sight of the blood trickling down my face. The car is in danger of stalling. I hold my hands out, fingers spread, sticky and red.

'This is real, Caro! How much more are you going to spill?'

'There's tissues in the glove compartment,' is all she says. She accelerates, eyes looking ahead, her mask back in place.

'You're mad, you know that!'

'I told you not to say that.' He taps me with the gun again, but gently this time, almost a caress. 'But maybe I am, little brother, maybe I am. Runs in the family.'

We're approaching the bridge now. They haven't finished working on it; the traffic is still single lane with temporary traffic lights across it. We get there just as the lights are changing. Caro slows right down, as if she is about to stop.

'There's only one thing left to do.' She breathes the words so quietly that only I can hear. Then she says: 'Get out of the car,' her voice low and deliberate. She says it again, loud and insistent, screaming the words in my ear. 'GET OUT OF THE CAR!'

I've got the door open and dive sideways, out of his line of fire. She speeds up, jumping the temporary lights which have just turned back to red. She has the long bridge to herself. She puts her foot down, the car picks up speed. Workmen turn, alerted by the roar of the engine, the squeal of tyres on tarmac. Then halfway across, just before the point where the stone parapet is replaced by a temporary barrier, she swerves hard to the left. The car mounts the pavement – workmen are shouting, scrambling to get out of the way. I hear the wooden barrier splintering, then a splashing roar as the car hits the river nose first and goes straight down.

For a moment there is silence, the only sound the lapping slop of the displaced water. Time seems to slow, then stop altogether so everyone is frozen in the moment looking towards the source of this extraordinary event, this disturbance to their lives. Then it all speeds up again and people are running, shouting for help, racing to the bridge. I scramble to my feet and I'm running, too.

I don't know what I expect to see as I get to the parapet. Maybe that she'll emerge. She's a good swimmer after all, a strong swimmer. Water is her element. She told me that. She will get out, people do escape from those situations. She will wriggle out and swim up to the surface. She will emerge from the water like a river mermaid – a nixie, a lorelei. She will appear any second. She has to survive. The prospect of her death does not seem a possibility. He'll come up after her. He's a born survivor. I cannot think of his death, either. He's been through a war – how could this kill him?

The seconds stretch to a minute, two. People hang over the bridge, line the bank, attracted by the drama, the spectacle. Unable to do anything, they lean forwards, straining towards the patch of disturbed water, point and gesture in a flutter of helpless hands. Time ticks by. The disturbance in the water has dissipated; the river resumes its flow.

36

I stay, staring down at the place, while emergency services arrive and the police begin questioning witnesses, wanting to know if anyone knew the identity of the occupants of the vehicle. I have a weird sense of shame, as though I've failed them. I lacked the power to stop them. I didn't have their guts, their courage. I couldn't live with either of them, or die like them. I am alive, I survived. I feel relief and guilt in equal measure and find I am crying, sobbing, and the tears will not stop. I see someone in the crowd point me out to a young policewoman. She comes over and asks me gently, 'What happened to you? Were you involved in the accident?'

I nod, unable to speak.

'Did you see what happened? Did you know the driver?'

I nod again, tell her my brother was also in the car. Tell her there is something else that they have to know.

She leads me by the arm to her senior officer. There's an inflatable recovery boat being brought down to the water, police divers checking their equipment. I have to stop them, warn them about the bomb. I think they won't believe me, but they take my warning seriously. The whole thing escalates from tragic accident to terrorist incident in an instant. Work is halted, the whole area is cordoned off, bomb disposal arrive. Divers are sent down. The car is brought up, it stands, shrouded in a white tent, the occupants still inside it, while experts work to defuse the bomb.

A paramedic sees to my cut, cleans me up, then I'm taken to the police station and questioned for a long time. I stick to my story that Caro was a hostage, we were both innocents with no idea what Rob was planning. No one will ever know for sure what sent them plunging into the river, but everyone believes that it was Caro, that she chose to sacrifice her own life to save others. It has turned her into a heroine.

37

I've put my words and theirs together. If there is any kind of explanation, then it is here. Rob posted his video diary on the Net. He's a hero to some people. It got a lot of hits before it was taken down. Caro's mother returned the rucksack that I'd left at her house. Caro's notebook was inside it, tied with red ribbon. On the cover, it says:

For You

I grieve for them every day, but really it isn't that simple. I'm angry with them for doing what they did, leaving early, leaving me to go on alone, and it'd be dishonest of me if I didn't admit to a little part of me that is thankful that they are no longer here to throw my life into turmoil, or to hurt me any more.

Writing this has made these feelings easier to

understand and to endure. *What you can't change, you got to live with*, that's what Grandpa used to say. I'll be living with this for the rest of my life. But at least I'll have a life. I'm ready now to say goodbye. The urn is heavy, heavier than you'd think, but a small container for a full-grown man. I take it down to the river. I choose to go in the very early morning, near dawn. I'm on the bridge, at the place where they went over, where the stone is paler. The light is soft. There's mist above the water. Down towards the weir, the river is rippling gold with the rising sun. I lean on the new stone of the parapet for a moment, looking down at the place where the water is still in shadow. I open the canister, tip it slowly and watch the ash drift in the slight breeze that always blows here, watch as the fragments fall and scatter, dimpling and dusting the dark surface.

In the little garden next to the bridge, I picked some roses. For her. Red and white and the palest yellow. She said, 'I don't do love,' but I think maybe she did. I let the petals flutter down to spread across the river, mingling with the ashes, to be taken by the restless current, borne away down the stream.